To Chloe
Love

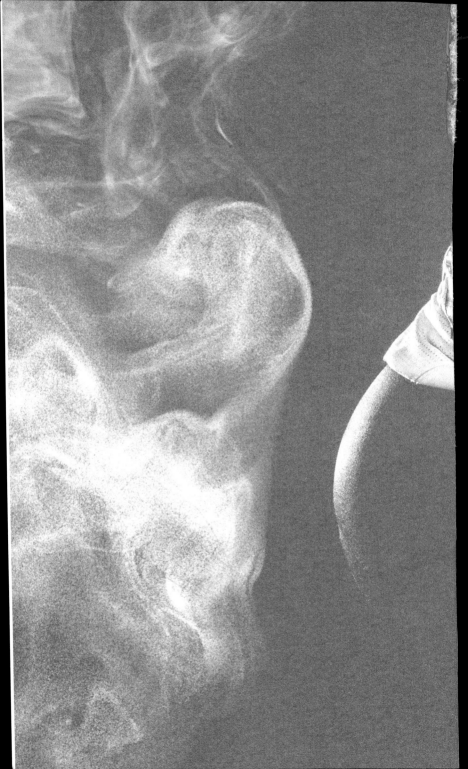

LINEBACKER

THE MONTANA LONGHORNS

T L WAINWRIGHT

LINEBACKER

By T.L Wainwright

Story Editor:
Nikki Young

edited by:
Caroline Stainburn

Cover:
Shower of Schmidt Designs

Second edition. June 2022
© 2022 T.L Wainwright
Written by T.L Wainwright

This is a work of fiction. The names, characters, places, and incidents are products of the writer's imagination or have been used fictitiously and are not to be construed as real. Any resemblance to persons, living or dead, actual events, locales or organisations is entirely coincidental. All rights reserved.

No part of this publication may be reproduced, distributed, or transmitted in any form or by any means, including photocopying, recording, or other electronic or mechanical methods without the prior written permission of the publisher except for brief quotations embodied in critical reviews.

Thank you.

T.L. Wainwright

LINEBACKER

One of the best and most versatile defensive players on the team due to their speed, strength, and size.

CHAPTER 1

"Pass the ball, numb nuts," I shout out, then take a step back into the shadow. "Shit Hope, you're an idiot." I reprimand myself under my breath. When I dare to step forward again, I'm thankful to see that despite my outburst, the noise on the field has masked it and hasn't given me away.

My father would pop an artery if he learned that the majority of the time when he thinks I'm studying in the library, I'm actually out here, feeding my addiction. I don't get to come to the games, only the practice and when I'm not under my father's scrutiny, I get to stream most of the NFL games on my phone but I have to do that once I'm in my bedroom with the sound down low. So, despite me hating every single member of the football team in front of me, I hide here in the shadows, getting my fix.

The British Universities American Football League (BUAFL) is tiny compared to its US counterpart and doesn't get the recognition either. But it's real, and I'm fortunate to go to one of the few high schools that has the sport on their curriculum. This is due to our American PE teacher, Dexter Blackmore, being an ex-Florida State University coach. Rumour has it he moved over to the UK for the love of his life, despite his devotion to the game. Guess his craving for the sport is as fierce as my own, because with sheer determination and perseverance, he brought his obsession for the game to a rather insignificant Yorkshire school.

After recruiting a dozen of half-interested students, who were starving for something new in their mundane life other than gaming, drinking cheap vodka and vaping, he got them to play out-of-school hours. Word of mouth was all it took before his love of the game spread to a ton of over sixteen lads. It was like a virus, and before he knew it, he had a pretty good line-up. The Head of the school couldn't ignore the fact that he had sparked fresh interest within the male pupils at the school and took it to the board. That was back in 2010, Since then they'd added American Football to the list of sports the school offered. The following year, Capa Down Academy boasted an impressive squad. The Capa Cobras were good enough to be part of a small but capable high school league.

"What the fuck, Bell?" I hiss as the quarterback Alfie Bell, who after getting the ball from the snap, tries to run it himself but almost immediately is sacked by Vance Marshall, otherwise known as Mars, tagged as the best defence linebacker in the league.

God, that must hurt.

Although Bell is a bit of a monster himself, he has nothing on Mars, a huge 6 feet 1 inch, 220-pound physique of pure hard muscle. With short cropped blond hair and grey eyes, Mars has a Nordic look about him. Slightly crooked strong nose, and generous, yet mostly in-expressive lips, you couldn't deny that he's a handsome dude. "Only got yourself to blame, greedy arsehole. You had options out there," I mumble, far from the usual acceptable sports commentary. "Both your wide receivers were open. Should have passed the fucking ball."

I let out a snigger as I watch Bell clamber to his feet and step up towards Mars, getting all up in his face. His body language shows how pissed he is at being sacked by his close friend. I can't help but enjoy the drama, knowing that these two so-called pals are butting heads. Although if it comes to blows, my money is on Mars. Bell is all piss and wind, but for some reason has a hold over the majority of the football team. While Mars is just as much an arsehole, he's more the silent but deadly, broody type. He doesn't need words, because the dark and dangerous glare he casts to those who cross him is enough to make the devil think twice about his actions.

A wave of disappointment washes over me when Coach Blackmore steps in between the two of them, giving them the hard word. I let out a vast sigh of frustration as the sound of their laughter carries on the breeze. I watch the two friends slap each other's back before they go in for a bro-hug.

The squad line up again to continue practice and I retreat further into the darkness in disgust, deciding that however much I love the game, I've seen enough of the fuckwit's camaraderie for one day. Too much bromance will only make me want to hurl.

As I'm here, I might as well put my free time away from my father's overbearing control to good use. I jog over to the door that leads back into the school, and the quickest way to get to the changing rooms. There are only fifteen minutes of practice left, and all the other teachers and pupils seem to have left for the day. It's only fair that I grasp the opportunity while I can.

The headmaster will no doubt still be here, but as his office is at the other end of the building where chances are, he'll be ball's deep in Candy Whitshaw, the six former he's shagging, I doubt he's going to be a problem. It's the worst kept secret ever. Even the department heads who are aware of his extracurricular activity seem to turn a blind eye. It makes me wonder what he's got over the rest of the teachers in this school.

I slip through the boys' changing room door, keeping one foot out in the corridor in case I need to abandon my mission. I hold my breath so I can hear. It takes a couple of seconds to listen for any sign that anyone is still hanging around in here, but when I'm met with complete silence, I make my move.

I should target someone else, but as Alfie Bell is the main instigator of my torment on the football team, I can't help but want to humiliate him the most. As I don't get many chances to take revenge, it's inevitable. He is on top of my list.

Bell's holdall stands out like a dick on a cake. It's expensive, pretentious and far from his out-of-work parents' budget. So, undoubtedly is nicked off one of the rich kids from year nine. I zip open the top, grimacing as I put my hand inside and rummage through the contents until I find the item that I'm looking for.

His boxer briefs have seen better days. The fabric of the crotch, not that I scrutinize it, is threadbare and one good fart could be enough to render them crotchless. I would have preferred an expensive pair to ruin. Calvin Klein or Armani. Nope, they're a supermarket brand, but they'll still serve their purpose.

With not much time to spare before the locker room will heave with testosterone-laden ball bags, I pull out a plastic bag from the zip pocket of my backpack. In it is a small jar of Nutella and a wooden stirring stick I gained from the coffee shop. With the grotty undergarment laid out on the bench, I twist off the top of the jar and, using the stick, mix up the contents until it becomes pliable. I scoop out a big dollop and spread it towards the rear of the pants until it looks like an enormous skid mark. On deciding to go all out, I add more, shaping it the best I can so it looks like the Bell-end himself got caught short and shit in his pants. To complete the prank, I lay the offending item across Bell's luminous, puke-green Nike trainers that he's so damn proud of, making it blatantly obvious who the soiled undergarment belongs to.

My shoulders shake as I force myself to hold in the rumble of amusement that's brewing in my chest. I place the half-empty jar and wooden stick back into the plastic bag and make a quick exit. The hall is still deserted thankfully. The last thing I need is to be seen anywhere near the boys' changing room. I take an alternative route towards the main school entrance so as not to risk coming face to face with any of the football team.

Best call yet, because when I get to where the hallway takes a right, I just make it around the corner before I hear footsteps and the unmistakable clicking of cleats hitting the tiled floor. I'm so tempted to hang around hoping to hear the reaction to the dirty pants, but it's too risky. I pick up my pace, making sure that I don't make a sound until I'm bursting out of the main entrance and down the steps. I drop the plastic bag containing the evidence on top of the already overflowing litter bin that hasn't been emptied since lunch break and walk away from the school.

CHAPTER 2

It's when I'm in the coffee shop's bathroom getting changed that I let myself go. The snorts of giggles that erupt from me burst out like lava, every muscle in my body shaking, wanting to be included in the celebration. But it's not long until the tears of laughter, that are now streaming down my face, morph to those of horror and regret at what I'd done. I've stooped to their level.

Although those arseholes have done nothing but give me shit since the day I turned up; the only female might I add, looking to join the football team. Hell, I didn't get anywhere near Coach Blackmore to even ask the question. They made sure of that by pushing and ridiculing me until they were determined that I had no other option but to leave.

"So why should I be remorseful?" I ask my reflection in the mirror, swiping away the wet tracks of my tears from my face. "It's time to give them shit back. I just have to make sure they don't see it coming."

As I stand in my underwear, I fold up my ripped black jeans, the well-washed 'The Pretty Reckless' band t-shirt and my second-hand biker jacket, which has so many cracks in the leather I'm surprised it hasn't broken apart and turned to dust. I put them away in the bag that I keep here, stashed in the manager's office.

Out of the plastic bag that had been resting on top of the holdall, I pull out an oversized, high neck, calf-length dress and reluctantly yank it over my head. I cringe at my reflection. The floral pattern is obnoxious. Like someone has just chucked up a night's worth of multi-coloured cocktails and thrown on a handful of dead flowers to mask the sickening smell. Although, all I can smell is mothballs.

Forced to wear old-fashioned clothing is bad enough, but that they belonged to my dead mother makes it twice as sickening.

A memory of my dear sweet mum jumps into my head. Pulled back hair, makeup free face, and a smile and brightness in her eyes that was only true for me. I smile to myself, but then it falls, and I shudder as I also recall how her expression would become fake, and her hand would shake as soon as my father appeared.

You see, my father controlled her every emotion and move she made, and it was entrenched in her that it was her job to keep me in line. Little did he know my mum did everything she could to make my life as normal as possible. She hid many things from him that no doubt he would have classed as immoral, an act against God's teachings. Like going to the cinema, because Satan himself lives in the popcorn machine, right!?

They were our secrets, and she had learnt to be a master of deceit. In the name of sanity.

That all changed the day she died, or should I say, the day she left, according to my father's side of the story. But I know the truth. I heard every forceful pounding of his fists that connected with my mum's tiny frame. I felt it mentally, along with the pain of not being able to stop or take them from her. I would have gladly been his punchbag on that day if I could have saved her, but I was trapped, locked in my room, unable to get free.

After removing the dark kohl from around my green oval eyes and the deep purple tint from my plump lips, I gather my long, naturally wavy dark hair and tie it back into a conservative ponytail. Last of all I detach the fake rings from my nose and bottom lip and place them in the inner pocket of the bag.

My reflection no longer shows my true inner identity.

I shake away the haunting memories from my bones and force myself to take on a lighter mood. With upturned lips, I swing my backpack over my shoulder and grab the holdall from the floor.

I find Windy, the manager, in her office. Her real name is Gail, but she hates it, so at a young age it was switched to Windy for obvious reasons and it has stuck.

"Hey, how was school today?" she asks as I stash the holdall in the back of the room where she lets me keep it. "Any trouble from the FUB's today?"

My tormentors, Bell, Mars, Smithy, Cocker and a few of the other football team, had been given that collective name by Windy after the first time she found me a blubbering mess in the Coffee shop bathroom. 'Fucking uneducated ball bags' was the term she used after I had relayed to her how they had cornered me at school. They had spouted how I was a weird, sad little bitch, with my blacked-up eyes, saying I looked like a corpse in my charity shop rejects. They were cruel, and it had been going on for weeks. The snide remarks when I passed them in the hallway. The accidental pushing and shoving.

Accidental my arse. What had started off as just an occasional comment had built up into relentless persecution.

Most of the time, I would ignore them, turn my back and walk away. But on that day, I'd had enough. Bell-end had snatched my bag, pulled out the contents and scattered them across the tiled floor of the hallway. He had then taken great pleasure in ridiculing me over the dress that was stashed in there, that I would need to change into before I got home. Two of them had held me still while he had forced it over my clothing. My chest had heaved with emotion, black tracks of tears had run down my face as he had dragged me up and down the corridor so that everyone could enjoy my embarrassment.

I was broken, ridiculed and a blubbering mess, but when he sniggered at the top of his voice so that everyone could hear. "Look at the state of you. No wonder your mum left you."

I exploded.

Bell didn't see it coming. I launched myself at him, my inner banshee coming to life. My fingernails were short because that's how my father insisted I kept them, but it didn't stop me from embedding them into his skin as I clamped my hands into each side of his face and smashed my forehead against his nose. Claret poured from his now misshapen nose; red beads of blood bloomed from where my nails had pierced his skin.

I'd drawn blood, and it felt fucking good.

Gripping my upper arms, he pushed me away, but I made him regret it. It gave me clear access to his dick, so I brought up my knee and slammed it right between his legs. His hands released me and went straight to his groin, then he hit the floor like the sack of shit that he is. It was at that point that his merry gang of arseholes came to their quarterback's aid, pulling me off of him as I went in with the boot. A teacher appeared before they got a chance to react further, giving me the perfect opportunity to escape.

Since that day, Windy had insisted I come here before and after school so that I can change from the god-awful clothing and into something that reflected my true self and not the image that my father wanted me to be. Windy's coffee shop had always been a favourite of Mums. She would bring me here for treats like chocolate milkshakes and double caramel brownies, which I would devour while she took her fill of double shot espresso. Whenever I get a waft of the strong aromatic drink, it prompts memories of her and how she would close her eyes and inhale the aroma before taking the first sip.

Windy had been one of the few people that had been a friend to my mum and this place has always felt like a safe haven. So, it was only natural after Mum's departure that I would gravitate here when I needed a place to go. I don't think that my mum ever spoke to Windy about Fathers' restraints and control over her, but from the way Windy looked and acted around her, yet never condescending, I'm sure that she had her suspicions.

"'Today was a good day," I respond with a dark undertone to my voice. It immediately has her dropping her pen as she spins her seat in my direction. Her eyebrows rise and hide under her thick, dark brown fringe that's as sharp as the shoulder length, poker-straight bobbed wig she wears today. Her inquisitive dark eyes focus on my face, noticing the smirk that I can't suppress from my lips.

"What have you done, girl?" she chuckles, with a wave of her hand. The purple and silver colour of her nails flashes and catches my eye.

"A little payback," I reply smugly. "But don't worry, I

made sure that I covered my tracks. Nice nails, by the way."

"I hope so, because your papa will go crazy if you get in trouble at school and you know I hate how he gets with you." She pushes the air out of her mouth through her teeth and hisses. "You know how much I'd love to go around there and kick his fake, righteous ass."

"But you also know that would make things worse. He'd take away my free time, which I only get because he thinks that I'm studying in the library and it benefits my education."

"I know, Sugar, but I hate that you have to stay under the same roof as that monster," she sighs out.

"Not for much longer." School's almost over, and once it is, that's when I'll plan my escape from him and his oppressive control.

CHAPTER 3

As I walk out of the room where I've just completed my very last exam, the sense of elation that washes over me has me grinning like a fictional cat. I can't help it. I can almost smell freedom and my mind becomes flooded with my getaway plan. As I make my way down the hallway, my head down so that I don't come across as borderline crazy, I pause when I hit a wall of hard muscle.

An 'Umph' noise bursts from my lips as all the air gets knocked from my lungs. I gasp for breath before mumbling out, "I'm so sorry." When the owner of the broad shoulders and toned back turns to face me, I see it is no other than Vance Marshall. "Oh, fuck."

Our eyes connect. The grey of his iris is flecked with brown and gold and the way they seem to flicker under the fluorescent lights is like peering into the universe. Mars takes a dramatic step back. His gaze burns into mine, his facial expression is of total disgust and annoyance from having touched me. Yet, he doesn't say a word, just glares at me, which kind of speaks volumes.

It's enough to have me taking a few steps back myself, but Bell quickly fills the space as he pushes in between us.

"Well, well, what do we have here?" he smirks down at me. As I'm only five feet three, it's not like I'm not used to people looking down on me. But this dick makes me feel like I'm dirt on his obnoxious, puke-green Nike's. "In a rush to get out of here, are we?" He sniggers. "Anyone would think that you were trying to avoid us."

I sidestep to go around him, only for him to mirror my action and block my way.

"What's the hurry, 'Hopeless'?" he fake smiles, using his favoured name for me.

I sidestep again, only this time it brings me nearer to the wall and when he copies me, he slams his hand against it. I sense rather than see someone move behind me, but I'm pretty sure because of the shadow that he's causing across Bell, it's Mars. I have nowhere to go now that I'm boxed in.

Flight is my usual go to reaction, but in this instance, that's not an option. For some reason, maybe it's the fact that in a few days I'll be away from this school, away from their mental bullying, harassment, and constant threat that hovers over me daily, I get an irrepressible urge to fight.

Hell, I'm still basking in the afterglow of my shitty pants prank, which was the talk of the school for over a week. Seems his football buddies didn't think twice about relaying that tale of his humiliation to the rest of the school, despite him being their QB1 king.

Could it be that Bell isn't liked as much as he thinks he is? That his teammates' loyalty has run its course and they are seeing him for exactly what he is. Me thinks that not everything is rosy in camp FUB and as his sheep will also flee the flock soon, their loyalty no longer holds much fortitude.

I take a step forward, losing the few inches between us. Tilting my head up, I look him straight in the eye and hiss, "Get out of my way, Bell-end," using my own preferred name for the arse wipe. With my feet six inches apart and planted firmly on the tiled floor, fisted hand resting on my hip, I growl out a further, "Move arsehole," I place my other hand firmly on his chest and push. I hope that my tone, stance and body language convey strength; enough to get the dick to back off. But when his hand curls around mine, which would have been a sign of endearment if it wasn't for the firmness of his grip, I realise that I'm failing abysmally.

"Jesus," he laughs, turning just enough so he can address the rest of his entourage as they hover around him. "Looks like my theory was right, lads. 'Hopeless' has been harbouring a crush on me all this time, and now that we're leaving, it's clear that her dreams of kissing me are and always will be just that. A fucking fairy tale."

"Ha, don't kid yourself, fuckface." I snigger in his face while trying to pull my hand out of his grip, but all he does is tighten it. "You might think you're all that, but from what I hear in the girl's bathroom, kissing you is like locking lips with a rancid lizard with a septic tongue." Two lads gasp but more of them laugh, some covering their mouths with their hands to stifle the noise.

All that does is egg me on, so I lean in a bit and take two exaggerated sniffs of the air between us.

"Do you know that brushing your teeth twice a day and a little mouth wash might help with the bad breath?" I say with all seriousness. "The dreadful, slimy lip action? I'll level with you. I'm not sure if that can be fixed." I yank again, harder this time to release my hand. When he lets go, I revel in the fact that I've won this particular tug of war, but when he spins me ninety degrees, pushing my back against the wall, it's short-lived.

"Lies," he spits. "And I'll prove it."

I'm not even aware that my mouth is open on a gasp, from the shock of being pinned against the wall until his lips are crushing mine and his tongue is halfway down my throat. Fact is, all my words were lies because I have no friends here and therefore not privy to any girl chat in the bathroom, hallway or changing rooms come to think of it. But I must be psychic or something because his kiss is vomit inducing and twice as bad as I'd described.

As he continues to ram his tongue in and out of my mouth, he gives me no option but to do one thing… bite.

As he pushes in, I clamp down. The coppery taste of blood tells me I've punctured flesh. It muffles his scream until I relax my jaw and push him away with all the strength I have. The blood that has collected in my mouth I have no desire to swallow, so I spit it at him. It lands on his shirt, on the exact spot where he had held my hand captive.

When he regains his balance, his fingers go to the corner of his mouth, then he pulls them away to examine the blood now coating the tips. The shock of my assault on him shows clearly on his face.

"You're a psycho bitch," he splutters. Blood and saliva dribble down his chin. His words are distorted, which tells me that his tongue is already started to swell.

"Maybe I am." I know that the smile on my face must appear like I've totally lost the plot, but I don't care. I feel violated. "Does that scare you, Bell-end?" With wide eyes and a lop-sided grin, I add, "Does it make you shit your pants?" The laugh that I exude is crazed, which only intensifies when I see the light of realisation explode on his face.

"It was you," he hisses out. His arms shoot forward and before I've had the chance to duck, his hand is around my throat, his forearm firm across my chest and my back once again slaps hard against the wall. Instantly, my hands go to his around my neck. Gasping for breath, I can sense my eyes are beginning to bulge, my fingers clawing against his hold as I try to get him to release the pressure.

"Enough," a deep voice roars from the side-line and the next thing I know, the pressure is gone and I'm on my knees panting and wheezing as I breathe in deep gulps of air. When I get my senses back and my vision clears, I raise my eyes to find that my tormentors are no longer crowding me. I do, however, catch sight of the retreating FUB's backs as they disappear further down the hallway.

My exams are over, so I have no reason to stick around for the rest of the afternoon. I get to my feet, hold my head up high, forcing down the signs of my pending breakdown, and walk. I ignore every single one of the students who stood glaring at me with smirks on their faces. Their eyes seem to burn into my skin as I make my way to the nearest exit. Not one of these vultures had stepped in to stop this when it had gotten out of hand. All they were interested in was the entertainment value. The last thing I'm going to do is let them get a kick from seeing my pain. I wait until I'm clear of the school grounds and view of anyone before I let my emotions come to the surface.

CHAPTER 4

go straight to the coffee shop because I'm shaking from the violence that has occurred, not only Bell's but my own too. I'm not in a fit state to go home.

As soon as I step through the door, Windy seeing the shaking, tear-stained wreck that I am, she's across the room and hustling me out the back and into her office. Once I'm sat in her chair, she rushes off. She's only gone a few minutes before she's back, kneeling on the floor in front of me, with hot tea that smells sweeter than a bag full of fudge.

"Drink this," she orders, placing the mug between my hands that are cradled in my lap. "Dear Lord, girl. What the hell has happened?"

My body shakes as I recited back to her the turn of events through trembling lips. By the time I've finished with the help of the hot, sweet tea, my emotions have turned from fear to anger. Fury bubbles through my veins, causing my hands to shake erratically. The fact that I had turned to violence to get back at them makes me sick to the stomach because it's not so different from the violence that I've seen and endured in my life and hate with a passion.

"I can't believe I did what I did," I exhale. "Do you think I'm like my father?"

"Hell, to the fuck. No." Windy fires back at me with a sharpness in her voice that I've never heard before unless referring to the FUB's. "You are nothing like your father. You were pushed too far and were retaliating, that is all."

Yes, the knee to his balls, a well know woman's go-to when being attacked, was brutal, but biting his tongue hard enough to draw blood. Fucking hell, what have I become?

"But that's not who I am. I can't fight them that way," I cry. "Don't get me wrong, I want to make them sorry, regret the hell that they have put me through for God knows how long, but not like this."

"Then we work smart." Windy stands to her full height in front of me. Moving to her desk, she grabs a notebook and pen from the top before resting her bottom against it. "Everyone has a secret or a weakness, an Achilles' heel, so to speak. All we need to do is work out what theirs is and hit them where it hurts without you actually being physical."

"Like what? It's not like I know much about their personal life."

"So, who are the players?" she asks.

"Jesus, Windy." I snigger. "They all are. Every one of them is on the team."

"I don't mean football player," she lets out a hiss of air from between her teeth. "As in, player with the ladies. Which ones have more than one girl on the go at one time? There must be at least a couple of them."

"Oh, I see what you mean now," I giggle with a vicious

undertone. "Well, you know how the entire team acts like it's America personified with the cheerleaders and all. Bell's the quarterback, so of course, he's dating the head girl, Trudy Baker." I can't contain the wild and wicked grin that plasters over my face and I feel a whole lot better. "But I overheard some girls talking and rumour has it he's been getting it on with her best friend, Mia Falls, behind her back."

"Really?" Windy sniggers. "Well, wouldn't that be a shame if it got back to this Trudy girl?"

"I'm not sure that's fair to the girls. I'm looking at getting back at the boys, not ruining any friendships."

"Mia ain't no genuine friend if she's shagging her so called best friends' boyfriend, now is she." Windy waved me off. "That's the number one rule in girl code. In fact, Trudy needs to know the truth, then she can decide whether Mia's a friend or a back stabber. Besides, I'm sure Bell will get his fair share of Trudy's wrath."

Windy scribbles a few words down on paper, before raising her head again. "What about the other guys? What can we do to piss them off?"

"The rest, I don't know that much about, other than them thinking they're superior to everyone else in the school just because they play for the Capa Cobras."

"What about the Linebacker, Marshall?" she asks.

"Mars? That big, thick lump of muscle's only interested in the sport," I huff out, shrugging my shoulders. When I think of him and try to pick out his negative points, it's more difficult than it is with some of the others. It's like he's so focused on football that he refrains from being the centre of my torment, having just enough presence to keep in with his mates but off the teacher's radar. "My impression of him is that he lives and breathes American football and couldn't care less about anything other than being on that field on game day and being the best when he is. I don't think he's ever missed a training session or a game. He's undoubtedly tight with Bell and wherever Bell is, he's right beside him. Mars never says or does much, but he's always there and seems to take great delight in watching me get humiliated."

"We could get him banned from playing. Slip some illegal steroid stuff into his bag, then tip off the school. That would get him suspended, maybe even kicked off the team," Windy sneered in a way that made me wonder where the hell this evil side had been hiding.

"I think that's going a bit too far. Besides, where would we get the drugs from?"

"True," she taps the top of the pen against her lip as she ponders.

"Laxatives," I suggest. "Not sure how I'd slip it to him, though. I'd never be able to get near enough to tamper with his food or drink."

"Do you think you could get into the changing rooms again without being caught?" Windy asks, her eyes light up with the idea that must have popped into her head.

"I guess so. I just need to time it right."

"Fiery Jack," she suggested. "Better still, Deep Heat Balm. You know that stuff that people use for muscle strains and aches. It heats up within seconds of being on your skin. You can get that as a roll-on, so you won't get it on your hands."

"And what exactly am I going to…" I stop talking because the look on Windy's face and the dark mischievous glint in her eye tells me what she's thinking. "His pants."

"You're damn right, girl," she laughs out loud. "I can

just picture his face when his balls are on fire. He'll be off that field before the start of the first quarter and running off to the shower to wash his meat and two veg."

"Bloody hell, Windy," I gasp out my surprise. "Anyone would think that you've done this before."

"What, taking revenge on an arsehole, or the heat treatment on a man's dick?"

"Either?" The smile on Windy's face gives me the answer I needed. "OMG, both? Oh, my word, you have done this before. Damn Windy, you're vicious."

"Believe me, Honey, the male species have wronged me more than once in my lifetime." Windy scribbles down in her book before snapping it closed and placing it on the desktop. "But I'll tell you something. Every single one of them regretted the day they underestimated me. Now, it's your time to do the same."

CHAPTER 5

Over the next few weeks, Windy helps me plan out several tricks. Trying to hit the entire team is hard, so I pick out the top five that I want to target. Mars, Smithy, Cocker, Daz and, of course, my nemesis, Bell.

We conclude that the perfect time to put our plans into action would be at the school prom, which is just over a week away.

There's only one exception, and that's Mars.

Today is the last game of the season and as luck would have it, it's being held at the JC Stadium in Leeds. At first, I think that all is lost as there's no way I could get out of the house long enough to get there and back. Never mind past both of the team's entourage and stadium staff and into the changing rooms. But Windy is a master planner and comes up with the perfect solution.

Dressed in conservative attire, Windy visited my father. After explaining that her respectable coffee shop was becoming busier day by day, she respectfully asked if he would consider allowing me to work for her. School was coming to an end, so a few hours in the evening wouldn't affect my grades and she'd pay well. Actually, she's willing to pay more, but she doesn't let on to my father so that at least I get to pocket some for myself. Windy goes on to say that if it works out for all of us, then there's an option of more hours once school is over.

Despite my father's reservations, I could see the pound signs in his eyes and a job nearer home where he could still keep a tight hold on me was too good an offer. He agreed. Little did he know that Windy's true motives were to get me away from his overbearing control and give me the time to put our plans into action.

On game day, I find myself in the passenger seat of Windy's Ford Fiesta, on our way to the JC stadium dressed in the staff uniform and clutching a very convincing counterfeit workers' access pass.

"So, exactly how did you get this?" I ask Windy, as I pull at the white polo shirt with the JC embroidered logo on the left breast pocket. The sweatpants are the real deal too, which makes me think that both items of clothing are a little on the hot side. "Did you nick them?"

"Damn girl," she barks, side-eyes me before she flicks her gaze back to the road ahead. "My friend's daughter, Lacy Wood, had a summer job there last year before she went off to university. She's been meaning to hand it back for months but never got around to it. I just offered to drop it in for her and she took me up on it."

"And what about the pass?" I ask, amused by Windy's corrupt versatility.

"That was easy." There's an element of proudness in the smile that lights up her face. "I scanned the pass and with a little jiggery-pokery, I switched the picture for the one I took on my phone the other day, then changed the name. I have a laminator that I use in the shop, so hey presto, a pass." Windy brings the car to a stop on one of the side streets a few hundred yards from the stadium. The surrounding streets are still quiet, but I'm sure they will fill up soon with parked cars and people making their way to the stadium entrance. But it's still early and the teams haven't even arrived yet. "The only thing I couldn't get was a lanyard."

I glance down at the pass and screw up my face at the name printed on it. "Stacy Woodcock."

"It's the best I could do, considering I had to work with the letters that were on there already."

"But… Cock?" I grimace.

"Actually, I thought it was appropriate when you consider the reason why we're doing this in the first place," she reasons with wide eyes.

"Cock's," we both say at the same time and burst out laughing.

"The more confidence you give off, the less chance you'll be challenged."

"Okay." I nod and shake out my shoulders to alleviate my simmering nervousness. "Are you still coming in to watch the game?"

"And pass up the chance of seeing Mars get his come-uppance?" She sniggers. "You bet your sweetness I am." She lays her hand across the back of my shoulder and pulls me to her for a hug. "Woo-hoo," she cheers, giving a little fist pump in the air. "Good luck. You can do this."

With a deep breath, a decided nod of the head, two toilet rolls stuffed up my t-shirt and the roll-on deep heat, I open the car door and step out onto the pavement.

I get all the way to the hall where the changing rooms

are without being noticed, until I move to the door with a decal for the Capa Cobras on it.

"Hey, what are you doing here?" the burly security guy stops me from pushing the door open. "The teams will be here any minute, so you can't go in there."

"I was told to bring extra loo paper," I said, waving the two rolls up in front of me. "I'll be straight in and out, promise."

"You're cutting it fine, lady," he grunts. I give him my best 'please sir or my boss is going to kick my arse,' pleading expression. "Make it quick."

"Thanks," I sing out and push my way into the room, praying that he doesn't follow me in.

You can tell that this is a big game for the Cobras, as all the uniforms are hanging up nice and neat above the benches that line two of the walls. Each named and numbered jersey is facing out, marking the players' allocated changing spot. A helmet sits on a shelf above, each one gleaming like new. Immediately my eyes are drawn to No. 54 Marshall. Under the pads on the bench below where his shirt hangs are a pair of football trousers, jockstrap and box. Boots are tucked underneath. I move the heavy pads to the floor, grab the Deep Heat from my pocket, and get to work. I haven't much time, so I quickly roll the ball on the leg of my pants until it's coated with the substance, then roll it on the inside of the box and jockstrap. There's a slight herbal odour from the balm, but I'm sure once the room is full of testosterone-filled arseholes, it won't be detected.

I jump at the loud knock on the door.

"What's taking you so long? The player-coaches have arrived, so they'll be here any minute."

"Coming," I shout back at security, and quickly put

everything back as it was. Before I open the door to leave, I drop the two toilet rolls into the huge recycle bin in the corner. No doubt it's there for all the empty plastic bottles of Gatorade that coach insists the team rehydrate on.

"Sorry," I say, stepping back into the hallway. "Someone left a floater in one of the cubicles. It needed a couple of flushes to get rid of it."

"What? Oh, okay." He doesn't question it any further but looks a smidgen guilty and confused, which makes me wonder if he had been caught short and had to pay a visit and was now questioning himself if he had been the one to have left something behind.

"Better get going," I say, walking backward. "I have to help cover the drinks kiosk." I spin around and dash down the corridor before I risk coming face to face with anyone that might recognise me.

"I don't understand," I groan out, now back in the car and making our way home. I swing my hands up in the air in frustration before letting them drop back into my lap.

"Girl, I'm just as confused as you," Windy sighed out. "Are you sure you got that stuff right into the box?"

"I put it everywhere, believe me."

What the hell?

We had watched, grinning and cackling like a couple of evil witches waiting for the sign that Mars had fire down below.

We got nothing.

Well, apart from an odd flinch and rearrangement of his package, which is nothing new. Most blokes have their hands down their own pants at least a couple of times a day. It certainly didn't affect his game. Much to our dismay. In fact, he'd played a blinder. Two interceptions and even took the ball into the end zone to score. In my eyes, he was the man of the match. "Maybe he's so focused that nothing will distract him from the game."

"Or he is insensitive to pain and that's why he hits as hard as he does. The perfect defensive player."

"Or his cock's dead," I snigger. "Fuck it," I curse, fisting my hand and punching the side of the passenger door.

"Hey, don't take it out on my car. It's done nothing to you." She chides. "We have to accept that this was an epic failure, but take comfort because we still have four more to get at and we will succeed." Windy pulls the car into her usual parking place at the coffee shop, turns off the engine and twists her body towards me.

"Prom." Holding out her clenched fist, she waits for me to respond. "Don't leave me hanging."

"Prom," I agree, bumping my fist with hers. "I can't wait."

CHAPTER 6

When I step through my bedroom door and out into the hallway, I can hear the whistling of the old stainless-steel kettle on the stovetop begin to subside. My father is up and I wonder what kind of mood he's in today.

"Good morning, Father," I call out as I move towards where he stands, pouring the boiling hot water into his favoured mug. *'I trust in god's goodness. Rom.8.28'* is embossed in thick gold lettering on the dark brown ceramic.

"Hope," he says, angling the side of his face towards me. I stretch up on my toes as far as I can to place a reluctant kiss on his cheek, but with the height difference, I end up hitting the very edge of his jawline. I draw on all my resilience to not show the shudder that threatens to unleash at my display of affection, which goes against my true feelings for him. Today, I need him to be in a pleasant mood.

"What would you like for breakfast today, Father? Sausage, bacon? Or I could make you your favourite, eggy bread?" I ensure that I don't call it French Toast, which I have done in the past just to get a rise out of him when feeling rebellious. He hates the French, Germans and the Americans. In fact, for a man who proclaims to be such a God-fearing person, you would think he would be more accepting.

"Eggy bread would be nice," he responds as he pulls out one of the old wooden chairs from under the worn red-topped, melamine table. The tone in his voice is lighter than I've heard in a long while. Maybe there is a God, and he heard my murmured pleadings last night.

I pull out a frying pan and light the gas on the stove. With a tiny drizzle of oil to coat the pan, I place it on the flame to heat while I grab what I need from the pantry. I break the eggs onto a plate, season with salt and pepper, then carefully so as not to splosh over the sides, whisk them with a fork. Once the mix is slightly bubbly, I cut two medium thick slices of bread from a loaf. I lay one slice on to the mixture, leaving it for about half a minute. After I lift and hold to let the excess egg mixture drip back on the plate, I flip it over to coat the other side. Transferring the egg-soaked bread into the now hot pan, it sizzles as it cooks. After a couple of minutes, I brown the other side. Once done, I lay it onto a clean plate and repeat with the second slice. When both are ready to eat, I finish it with a small drizzle of ketchup across the now crispy French toast.

"This looks good," my father acknowledges when I slide the plate, knife and fork in front of him. "Are you not having some?"

"I'm going to have yogurt today." I'm not hungry, but I don't fancy a lecture about how food is integral to communicating the biblical message and the rest. My lack of appetite could be down to nerves, but I grab a carton of natural yogurt from the fridge anyway and hope that it's not gone past its sell by date. That would only spur on another rant from my father about waste and God's starving children around the world. I wonder if he would see it the same way if the only starving children were French?

Hypocrite.

We sit in silence. My father chews every morsel of his food like it's a sacred offering, while I almost gag on each mouthful of sour fermented milk.

"Father," I singsong, finally plucking up the courage to ask the question that has me so on edge. "It's the school prom next Friday and, well, all the other six formers will be going." I've toyed with the idea of telling him that I'm needed at the coffee shop to help Windy with a deep clean. But that would be another lie and, to be honest, I'm sick of them. It's time I start to stand my ground.

Despite the bunching of his eyebrows and the deep crease that has appeared between them, when he verbally responds to my request, his tone of voice is light and surprisingly has no sign of annoyance.

"Not all," he replies once swallowing his mouthful of food. "Because you, my child, will not be attending."

"But Father, teachers will be there to chaperone, so there won't be any drinking or smoking. Just music and dancing and I promise I'll leave early and be back by ten," I plead, my voice pitching higher and higher with desperation. "I know I don't have many friends at school, but it would be nice to have this last memory of my school years." I would love to have the type of relationship with my only parent where I could blurt out the real reason I needed to attend, but that wasn't happening, was it?

"Hah! The teachers at that school have no morals, and can't be trusted," he snorts before becoming more serious. "I will not allow a daughter of mine to gallivant around with a bunch of sexually deviant, young boys and promiscuous, immoral girls who have no respect for our lord or his teachings."

"I'm eighteen now, Father and in the eyes of the law, I'm an adult."

"In this house, I am the law, and I say no." He shouts, his temper rising to a point where his face contours into something dark and scary. "That's the end to it."

"But Father," I try again, knowing that I'm pushing my luck. The chair he was sitting on flips back and hits the floor as he jumps to his feet. He leans over the table; his hand snaps out and slaps me hard across the face.

I bite down on my bottom lip to hold in the cry that's lingering on my lips, determined not to give him the satisfaction of seeing my pain. My cheek burns and the side of my head throbs from the impact, but I clench my hands firmly in my lap, rather than using them to soothe away the pain.

"I said enough," he sneers at me. "One more word and I'll beat the defiance out of you with my bare hands. Now get to school before I make good on my threat."

I get to my feet, grab my bag, and slip on my old worn shoes before bursting out of the front door and out into the morning sun.

"Happy fucking birthday to me," I shout out once I'm far enough from the house and no one is around to hear my outburst.

School is not where I need to be today, but I'll be damned if I'll make my father aware of that. All of my exams are complete, so I only need to be there on the last day. But the thought of having to spend more time at home is unbearable. Instead, I make my way to Windy's and the only person who will want to celebrate and acknowledge the significance of today. And the person who will help me find a way to get my night at the school prom and ultimately my revenge.

CHAPTER 7

wait until nine in the evening, the time we always retire to our respective rooms for the night. Father's rules. Up before 7 am. Bed by 9 pm. He's a stickler for it.

Most of the time when I'm in my room I read or find an NFL game to watch on my phone until I drift off to sleep. But tonight, I'm slipping out of the window with my backpack full to bursting, dressed all in black like a cat burglar.

Once I'm a safe distance from the house, I jog towards school. The dance started at 7 pm but is due to go on until 11 pm, so although I'll be arriving late, it will still give me plenty of time to put my plans into action.

They hold the prom in the huge sports hall and when I get to the front of the school, much to my dismay there's a group of students all dressed up in gowns and suits hanging around the entrance.

"Ah fuck," I curse under my breath as I hold back in the shadow of the extensive building, so I'm not seen. I wait for a while hoping that they are going to move back inside, but time is ticking away, and I need to get going.

A loud bang sounds out behind me, that seems to be coming from further down the side of the building, I creep towards it, expecting to see someone making out or something. What I find is one of the fire doors propped open with an old brick and the ground littered with butt ends. There's a distinct smell of cannabis lingering in the air. Their bad conduct had just saved my skin and given me an alternative way into the building.

Once I've slipped through the door undetected, I make my way towards the far end of the corridor that runs toward the front entrance. Halfway down there's a storeroom where the caretaker keeps his stuff. Ladders, buckets, the usual shit. It's the perfect place for me to change and stash my bag. I jimmy the locks in no time at all and hurry inside.

It doesn't take me long to switch out of my black clothing and replace them with a red, fitted dress, and matching shoes I have stashed in my backpack. The fabric of the dress clings to my body, especially my tits and arse. The hem is short and barely covers my decency. The five-inch heels make my legs appear to be super long. The extra few inches in height also gives me the confidence and sass that I need to pull this off.

With the tiniest of mirrors, I add a little drama to my appearance. Smokey eyes, eyeliner that goes all the way over my eyelids and then tapers to a line that makes my eyes seem more cat like. My eyelashes are naturally long and thick, but I enhance them a little more with black mascara. Peachy, pink blush and a deep red lip colour complete the look. The final touch is a platinum blonde wig from Windy's collection. The straight as a die fringe, and the poker straight bob, that rests just past my jawline, couldn't be more different from my usual almost black, long and unruly natural hair. I gasp at my reflection it the tiny mirror. I look so different. I can't deny that, with the way the dress hugs my body and the dark, sultry make-up that I would never have pulled off if it wasn't for Windy's patient instruction and a couple of YouTube tutorials, I feel sexy as fuck.

After I stash my bag in the storeroom's corner, I slip back out into the corridor and make my way to the sports hall.

When I get to the entrance of the room, the first thing I see is the large black and white archway made of balloons. No doubt where the photographer would have taken the customary photo of all the coupled-up pupils as they'd arrived. How vomit inducing. Another bonus to turning up late is the photographer has done his job and gone. Well, it's not like the school would pay for him to hang around any longer than necessary, especially at the risk of him catching less than savoury pictures once the night moved on and the kid's got rowdy.

It's amazing how the hall has been transformed for the event. The walls are covered with alternating white and black silky fabric from top to bottom. The ceiling has been given the same treatment, only they've draped the fabric like sails, making the entire room seem like a giant monochrome Arabian tent. A glitter ball that sits slap bang in the centre of the ceiling is a little understated and I can't help but think a chandelier would have been more fitting.

Glossy tiles cover the floor like an enormous chest board keeping in line with the black and white theme to the party. Balloon displays in the same colours are placed in each corner and around the edge of the room along with tables and chairs. Some are taken, some empty. A couple of dozen single balloons mingle amongst the gyrating bodies that are already on what seems to be the nominated dance area. Everyone looks to have stuck with the colour dress code, but not me.

In this instance, I want to stand out from the crowd. Besides, I've never been the type to dress in the latest fashion. I've always looked different from the rest, even if it had made me a target for the bullies. Me, I'm more Rock Chick than It Girl. That's when I'm not forced into dressing in chintzy old people's clothes and I get to be me.

They are all sheep, and it proves my point when one by one, their heads turned to the girl in the red dress. Even though my nerves are as jumpy as the rapid beat of the music, I walk towards the drinks table to the left of the dance floor which takes me past some of the busier tables, with all the poise and confidence of a catwalk model.

It's clear by the looks of some of them that not all the drinks that have been consumed tonight have been as per the no alcohol rules. That, along with the pot smoking, benefits me as it's clear that none of them seem to recognise me. Exactly what I was banking on.

After grabbing a drink from the makeshift bar, I scope out the room looking for my first target. There she is, Mia Falls and my luck is in, she's stood at the edge of the dance floor by herself watching and laughing at a couple of her friends doing slut drops on very unsteady legs. I walk over to her and tap her lightly on the shoulder.

"Hey, are you Mia?" I shout, trying to make myself heard over the noise of the music.

"Yes," she twists to face me with a smile which quickly drops and is replaced with straight lips and raised eyebrows. "Who are you?"

"I'm Alfie's cousin. Don't tell anyone, but he snuck me in," I offer, giving her a pleading look. "Anyhow, he asked me to tell you to go to the boys' changing rooms. I think that's what he said." I shrug my shoulders and nibble my finger that's resting against my bottom lip, then pull it back so she doesn't notice the half-chewed nail. It's not like it goes in line with the rest of my disguise and I hardly had time to stick on any falsies now, is it?

"He said if you wait there, he'll meet you as soon as he can get away."

"Really?" she beams back at me, a wave of guilt washes over me for involving her. But hey-ho, she is doing the dirty with her best friends' boyfriend. The next minute she has her arms wrapped around me, hugging me. "Thanks, and don't worry, I won't say a word about you being a gate crasher." Jesus, I'm such a bitch and for a second, I consider telling her it's all a lie. But only for a second.

"Thanks," I reply releasing myself from her hold. "Now go, otherwise you might miss him."

As soon as her back has disappeared out of the room, I hunt down Bell hoping that he hasn't got his girlfriend, Trudy, hanging around him like an unpleasant smell. I strike lucky again when I find a group of the football team and as predictable as always, Bell is playing centre stage to them all. As soon as he sets eyes on me, a mischievous smile plays on his lips. At first, I think he's recognised me, but when he swaggers over to me. It's then that I realise it must be his attempt at a flirty smile.

Catastrophic failure.

How the hell did this fucker manage to snag girls like Trudy and Mia. Yes, they might be A-typical popular girls and have their heads up their own arses, but no one could ever deny that they're both gorgeous.

"Hey, pretty girl," he creeps. Coming to my side, he

slides his arm across my shoulders. "Are you Cinderella, because if you are, you've just found your Prince Charming."

Vomit!

"Really?" I gasp, shrugging out from his hold and scowling at him. "Is that the same pickup line you used on my cousin, Mia?"

"Mia's cousin…" he spluttered. "Of course. It was a joke. I know who you are," he laughs nervously. "Mia said you'd be coming tonight and well, with the description she gave me, I knew it was you."

God, I can smell the bullshit and I bet it tastes nothing like Nutella.

"Well, Mia says she needs to talk to you."

"Yeah?" he glances around the room to see if he can pinpoint her. "I'll catch up with her in a bit."

"She said it was urgent. Said something about if you didn't go, then I had to find her friend Trudy instead," I add trying to make it sound like it's something he shouldn't miss.

"Where is she?" he questions his brows bunched together. Probably worried that she going to drop a pregnancy bomb or something. He looked like he might lose his shit. Worried that I might be handling this all wrong I decide to switch tactics a little.

"She's waiting for you in the boys' changing rooms," I smile salaciously. I cock my hip and top it off with a wink. "She said she had something real special for you."

"Hey guys," he hoots towards his mates. "I just need to go sort someone out," he winks at them, his tongue pushing into the inside of his cheek to emphasize the message. "I'll be back soon."

He doesn't acknowledge me further, not now he has

the promise of getting his end away. I wait until I'm sure that he's making his way in the right direction before I follow him at a safe distance. Once he enters the room and the door has swung closed behind him, I go to stand outside the door.

I can hear their muffled voices, and by what I can make out, Mia is already down to her underwear and waiting for him.

"Damn girl, are you that desperate for the arsehole?" I mutter under my breath before I turn to return to the hall.

The next part of the plan is all to do with timing. Unfortunately, I have to visualise in my head Mia and Bell-end getting it on so I can roughly work out when they would be in the most… compromising position. In other words, fucking. But as I get nearer to the hall, I see Trudy Baker disappearing into the female toilets. I wait a few seconds before I follow her in. By the time she comes out of the cubical and starts laboriously washing her hands like a germaphobe in a chlamydia clinic, I worry that I'm running out of time.

"Excuse me," I interrupt once I finish reapplying my lipstick. "You're Trudy, aren't you?"

"Yes, so?" she said with a resting bitchface.

"Aw sorry, you might not know who I am. I'm here with one of the other members of the football team, I'm Smithy's girlfriend." I pick him not for any other reason than as far as I'm aware he's not dating any of the girls in school. "He sent me in here to pass a message on to you from Alfie."

"Ah, decided that I'm worthy of his attention now has he, after he's been ghosting me most of the night?" she sneers. "Well, for once he will just have to wait."

"Hey, don't shoot me, I'm just the messenger. But

according to Smithy, he's organised something special, and he's waiting in the boys' changing rooms for you."

"Jesus, the changing rooms. So not fucking romantic," she complains but her eyes are lit up with excitement at what he could have planned. "Might as well go check out the dickhead," she huffs out, throwing her lip gloss back into her clutch bag and snapping it closed. Another one with no manners, she tucks the bag under her arm and walks out of the bathroom without a please or thank you. Well, kiss my arse!

I follow her at a discrete distance because, hell, I sure don't want to miss the shit show that's about to go down. That is if my plans worked.

Before the door has closed behind her, an ear-piercing shriek travels out into the hallway. I slide up closer so I can hear it going down. Trudy's high pitch hysteria is so distorted by her anger I can't quite make out every word. But the gist of it is that although I hope for her to catch them fucking, my timing was out. Seems that Trudy had caught Mia sucking Bell's cock. Not exactly what I wanted but when Bell shouts out at the top of his voice, "It's not what it seems," followed by "she came on to me, she wanted it," I can't help but grin. Crashing sounds come next, followed by a few ouches and fucks from the Bell-end himself and I'm already chalking this one up as a win. The voices inside become louder and closer to the other side of the door, so I make my retreat. Fast. But only to a place where I can continue to watch the events unfold.

Bell comes out on a sprint almost tripping over the legs of his pants that he hasn't quite managed to pull back up. Trudy is right behind him cursing up a storm using language that is far from what you would expect to come out of such a pretty mouth. But then again, I know however much she tries to put on an air of class, she's nothing but a prissy, pretentious princess from the local council estate. LOL!

Mia comes out next, stumbling behind them while trying to straighten out the puffy skirt of her dress. Her cheeks are red, clearly from both her embarrassment and the lipstick that has travelled from her mouth and, chances are, also damning evidence on Bell's bell end. It's a shame that I'm the only spectator but Capa High is no different to any other school. However much Bell will try to stifle the gossip, it will spread like herpes in a whorehouse, and for him, it will be like swimming against a tsunami.

I bring my index finger to my mouth, lick it, strike it in the air and think to myself, *'one down, three to go'*.

When I get back into the main hall, Bell and Trudy are screaming at each other in the far corner. Mars, Mia and the rest of Trudy and Bells groupies are hanging on the side-lines watching the whole thing as it unfolds. Problem is, my three remaining targets are amongst them.

The rhythm and beat of the music that's playing is perfect, so I make my way into the centre of the dance area, which at the moment is thin on takers because they're more interested in the Bell and Trudy show.

The only dancing that I've done before has been in the privacy of my bedroom. I'll admit that I've stood in front of the mirror while watching Beyonce on YouTube, trying to mimic her sexy moves. Well, I need to get their attention, which one, I'm not bothered, but it's time to shake my stuff and hope it works.

CHAPTER 8

With my hands held high above my head, I sway and gyrate my hips as seductively as I can. The beat changes to a slightly slower tempo, so I bring my arms down, running the palms of my hands over my breast and onto my hips. When I sense someone up close behind me, I tilt my head so I can check out who it is and bingo, it's Smithy. I glance forward again and find Cocker is here too. He's stood right in front of me swaying to the music, only a couple of inches are between us. He takes a few steps forward as Smithy's body becomes flush with my back. Fuck, it's like I'm the filling in a fuckwit FUB sandwich. I gulp down the urge to punch them away. Instead, I put my hands around Cocker's neck, and arch my back so that my tits hit Cocker's chest. In turn, my arse makes contact with Smithy's crotch all while I continue to sway my hips. Fuck, it must be working because there's a prominent hardness pressing into the base of my back, and when I look down Cocker's pants are tented at the front.

Woah! I'm well out of my comfort zone. Yet, I have a

sick sense of satisfaction that I, 'Hopeless' Harper, *'snigger'*, has them both hard and wanting me. Or should I say the sexy blonde version of me in the fiery red dress?

I go up onto my tiptoes, lace my hands into the back of Cocker's hair, and pull him down towards me. His eyes drop down to my lips, but kissing him, that's not happening. I tilt my head to the side until my mouth is against his ear. I'm just about to suggest going somewhere more private when he's yanked back away from me. I take a few seconds to comprehend what's going on, but when I see the tall figure in front of me, with a face of utter ferocity, fear hits me.

"Father?" How is he here? How would he know where to find me? What the!?

The grip on my arm is so tight that my skin tingles from the cut in my circulation. Lifting me until I'm almost off my feet, he brings me up to his level.

"Home. Now," he sneers into my face, his spit peppers across my cheeks. I trip more than once, my feet barely keeping up with his pace. I would have fallen several times if it wasn't for his tight hold on me. He drags me through the balloon archway, out into the hall and towards the exit doors.

The doors slam shut behind us. The cold air hits my heated skin and only adds to the shivers induced by my complete and utter fear of the savagery that I see in my father's eyes.

"I'm sorry, Father," I blurt out, hoping that if at least I show remorse he might go easier on my punishment. When we get to the bottom of the steps that lead up to the school entrance, he comes to a sudden stop.

"Whore," he screams in my face. "You dirty, filthy whore. I saw you with those two boys."

I don't need to look behind me to know that already an audience has followed us out and are congregated at the top of the stairs watching. Guess the Bell and Trudy show has gone down in the ratings. A new soap opera is now grabbing their attention.

"It's not what you think, Father," I plead, tears spill from my eyes from pain, fear and embarrassment. "If you'd just let me explain."

"I haven't time to listen to your lies," he spits back. He looks to the sky, adding "The Lord sees and knows what you have done."

"Father, I have done nothing. Please just listen to me."

"Not done anything?" he laughs hysterically, "I find you here after you've defied my orders, only to find you dressed like some common harlot. Dancing with not one but two of Satan's disciples. You give me no option but to punish you as the Lord would find fit for your despicable debauchery."

"No," I screech back at him. I bring back my free hand and whack my father across his face. But when I pull as hard as I can against his restraint, hoping that the shock of my retaliation would give me the chance to get away, he increases the pressure of his hold until my bones feel like they might snap. "Let go of me!" I screech out from the pain that pulses up my arm to my shoulder, so painful that bile rises into my throat. I swallow, not wanting to show weakness. The air between us is highly charged with hostility but the ever-growing crowd that watches as the drama intensifies only fires up my determination. "I said let go, Father."

"You little bitch." My father pulls back his hand ready to strike me and my body tenses up anticipating the impact. But suddenly he hesitates when a dark shadow falls over us.

"Sir," a deep throaty voice vibrates from behind me. "I don't think this is the place to air your domestic issues." I don't need to turn my head to see who it is but, I do anyway. Mars stands, legs apart, feet firmly planted on the flagstones close behind me.

"And who might you be?" my father grunts at the enormous figure that's dared to interrupt our altercation.

"I'm Mr, Marshall," Mars replies. He's tall, big and dressed in a dark grey suit. His tie is still in place, and with the dark stubble that is already showing on his face, he looks more man than boy. "Head of the science department. You must be Mr. Palmer. I don't think we've met before." Mars holds his hand out to my father, and as the hand that my father needs to respond to his gesture is the one that is holding on to me, he has no option but to release his grip.

As soon as Mars has my father's hand in his, he squeezes it tightly then punches him straight in the face. "That's for Hope." Mars sneers before he releases him. My father's hands instantly go to cover his mouth and nose, and blood gushes between his fingers.

"Time to leave, Hope," Mars instructs firmly and grabs my hand. He threads his fingers through mine and quickly pulls me away. We take off running. The sound of my fathers' pain rings out as he shouts and splutters my name. But I don't take any notice, I just keep on moving.

"Where are we going?" I pant out as we run across the grass verge towards the parking area. He's about to answer when I stumble as my heel becomes stuck in the soft grass, but Mars picks up on it instantly and comes to a stop. He bends down, slides my foot out of the stuck shoe and pulls it loose from the soil before he hands it to me.

"Hold on tight," he orders as he scoops me up into his arms and sets of running again. "My car is over there," he replies as clear as day, no sign of the fact that he's sprinting across the school grounds while carrying me. "After that, fuck knows."

He drops my feet to the floor when we arrive in front of a white Range Rover Evoque and moves around to the driver's side. Me? I stand there not quite knowing what to do.

"Come on," he laughs. "What are you waiting for? Get in."

"Is this yours?" I question not sure how an eighteen-year-old can afford such a big, fancy car. When the image of my father's angry face flashes to the forefront of my mind, I no longer hesitate and jog to the passenger side to get in. I slide onto the black leather, plush seat, to find Mars is already seated with his belt firmly in place. The engine roars to life.

"I stole it, but don't worry, I put fake number plates on." My mouth drops open and my eyes glare at him over the centre console. "I'm joking," he sniggers flashing me a look that I can't quite decipher. It's not like I've seen many other expressions on his face other than serious. "It's my mums but as she's out of town, I get to use it. You might think I'm a bit of an arsehole, but I sure as hell aren't a thief."

Silence falls between us as Mars drives us out of the school grounds. When we've put a few miles between us and the shit storm we left behind, Mars breaks the stillness within the car.

"Must admit, I never would have imagined you as a

blonde and I was curious why you'd turn up dressed as you did, but now it all makes sense."

"Shit!" I curse out. "I left my bag in the storeroom. I have to go back."

"No way am I taking you anywhere near your crazy arsed father," Mars growls, his ginormous hands gripping the steering wheel so hard that the skin at his knuckles turns white.

"Then let me out here and I'll walk." His head snaps around. No longer is he looking at the road ahead but casts me a dark glare. "Mars, I need my backpack. It has important things in there so, I need to get it back. Period."

"What can be more important than avoiding the risk of coming face to face with your dad? Who, by the way looked like he was about to beat the living shit out of you."

"Things, my things." However much I try to hide my building emotions from him, the crack in my voice gives it away. "Pictures of my mum are in there."

"Your mum, who left you?" he questions but I don't sense that he's being judgemental in any way.

"My mum didn't leave. He killed her."

"What?" Mars gasps before slamming on the brakes. As my body jerks forward with the sudden motion, Mars slings his arm comes across my chest, gently guiding me back into my seat. "He. You mean your dad? Jesus. I don't believe it."

"You saw how he was with me, is it that hard to comprehend?" Shit, what am I doing? I've lived with this secret for years, protected my father, played along with the lie, so why now am I spilling my guts to someone who is, for all intents and purpose, my enemy? "Never mind," I snap, jerking the door handle trying to get it to open so I can get out of here. "Can you please open the door?"

"Hey, stop." Mars leans across to my side of the car and catches my hand that is still trying to release the door catch. "If you tell me where it is, I'll go get your bag."

"You will?" I gasp out. Relief floods through me.

"Only if you promise to stay in the car, okay?" He searches my face for a sign of my acceptance, concern etched in his eyes.

"Yes, yes, I promise."

The car pulls forward and at the first opportunity Mars makes a U-turn and we head back towards the school.

While he concentrates on the road ahead, I explain where I stashed my backpack, which closet, right in the corner at the back and behind the floor polishing machine. When he brings the car to a stop about a quarter of a mile from school, I panic, thinking that he's changed his mind. But he turns off the engine, opens his door and jumps out.

What the hell is he doing?

"Why are you stopping here?" I ask as he stands with the door wide open and shrugs out of his jacket.

"Can't risk going any closer in case your dad is still hanging around. By now he will have realised that I'm not who I claimed to be and will have reported it to the teachers. I can run the rest of the way, and hopefully be able to slip into the school, grab your bag and make it back without being seen."

"Try the fire exit down the west side," I offer, giving him the option to take the same route in that I used myself. "It's the nearest one to the closet and hopefully no one has noticed that it's open yet."

"Yet?" he queries.

"Guess it's the nominated smoking area. Someone had

propped it open so they can come and go without being detected."

"So, that's how you slipped into the building unseen." With a nod of his head, he glances down the street towards the school. When he snaps his gaze back at me he cracks a smile, his full lips open and he gives me a flash of perfect white teeth. Even in the limited light of the interior it's unmissable. "Clever girl," he chuckles.

"How do you…" Before I get the chance to finish my question he's closed the door and all I see is his broad, imposing figure moving in front of the car and onto the pavement. I keep watching until he takes the corner and disappears out of sight. "… know that I didn't walk through the front doors like everyone else?" I finish my sentence although he's no longer here to answer.

CHAPTER 9

We've been driving for about an hour before Mars pulls the car up outside a Travel Stop hotel off the M1, just outside Sheffield.

After explaining to Mars that I have no family to speak of other than an aunt in London, we toyed with the idea of going to the coffee shop or Mars's house seeing that his parents were out of town. We decide both options were too risky as they would be the first places that my father and the teachers would look.

I then came up with the idea of driving out of the area and finding a cheap hotel to hide out for the night. I had some money in my bag that I'd been saving from my shifts working with Windy, so as long as it wasn't the Hilton, then I could afford it, just this once. Mars agreed and followed the signs for the motorway bringing us here.

When I move to get out of the car, Mars lays a hand on my arm, holding me back.

"Let me go in first," he suggests. "See if they have a room available."

"I can do it," I grumble back at him, as I jerk away from his hold. "I'm not a charity case, Mars. I do have money."

"Hey," he gasps back at me holding his hands up in submission. "That's not the reason I offered. The fewer people that see you the better. Plus, I'm a big motherfucker, and look older than I am and less conspicuous. You, no disrespect but despite the dress, makeup and wig, still look young."

"I'm the same age as you, arsehole," I grumble back at him.

"Sure, but I fooled your dad into thinking I was a teacher." He has a point. "Besides, do you have a credit card, because chances are they won't let us secure a room without one?"

"Okay, but I'll give you the money," I bark back at him.

"Jesus, let's just see if we can get one first then we can discuss the finances later," he chides back, "Wait here and I'll be back in a bit."

Luckily for us they have availability and we manage to sneak past the reception area, down the corridor and into the room undetected. The last thing we need is for people to become suspicious of the very young couple, turning up at a cheap hotel late at night with no luggage. God knows only too well what assumption they will come to.

When you consider the cheapness of a night's stay the room isn't that bad. It consists of a double bed, open wardrobe, desk area with a TV and a couple of chairs. The bathroom houses a walk-in shower, toilet and sink. The main thing is that it's clean, although the towels have seen better days.

After I dump my backpack on to the bed both Mars and I stand in the centre of the room shrouded in uncomfortable silence.

"Can you ditch the wig?" he asks when he eventually speaks. "It's a little off-putting."

"Don't you like it?" I play with the tips of the platinum hair, raising an eyebrow at him in question.

"It's not you, that's for sure. But I must admit, it pretty much fooled them all."

"But not you?" I slide the wig off of my head along with the net cap that was holding my natural locks flat to my head. I fling it on top of my bag before running my fingers through my hair and giving my itchy, warm scalp a good scratch. How the hell Windy wears these things I'll never know.

"Maybe at first, but I had this weird feeling that I knew you from somewhere, something was familiar."

"So, what was it that gave me away?"

"The way you stand with your left shoulder slightly forward and the tilt of your head," he explains like it's blatantly obvious. "The main giveaway is when your start nibbling on your little fingernail like Doctor Evil."

"Who the hell is Doctor Evil?" I scoff, as I drop and sit at the bottom of the bed.

"Don't tell me you've never watched the Austin Powers' movie?" he puffs out a laugh as he takes a seat beside me. His firm muscled arm brushes against mine, and I'm zapped by static electricity. We both intake a sharp breath, making it clear that I'm not the only one who felt it. "It's a classic and one of my favourites," Mars adds, his voice unusually higher than the norm.

"Well, I don't watch a lot of TV," I retort. Truth is we don't have one but I'm not about to admit to that.

Suddenly, something occurs to me. Mars had recognised me in my slightly slutty getup simply by my body language, even though I was trying to act like someone else. No one else had picked up on it, even though they notice me well enough when they want to torment me. Mars had actually seen me. What does that mean? I sure as hell don't know but I can't ignore the warmth that blooms on my cheeks or the flutter in my stomach. I should say something, but I'm lost for words.

"Don't know about you, but I'm hungry," he says jumping up suddenly and moving towards the door, which makes me wonder if he's noticed my embarrassment. "Do you want something?"

"What I really want is to get this stuff off my face." I swipe the back of my hand over my mouth and when I look down it's stained with red from my lips. "And this stupid dress."

"I wouldn't call it stupid," he mumbles under his breath but not quietly enough that I don't catch it. I think he realises that too by the way he shifts awkwardly on his feet. "Tell you what, I'll go grab what I can from the vending machine I saw when we came in. While I'm gone, do what you need to do. I have some spare clothes in the boot of the car. I can grab them but they'll drown you."

"No need, I have some stuff in my backpack," I smile shyly at him. "In fact, I'm going to take a quick shower, so I'll take it in with me."

"Okay, well I'll take the key card with me so I can let myself in, in case you're not done when I get back."

"Great. Oh, and I wouldn't mind a coke if they have any. I've got money." I pull my backpack towards me and go to the front zip pocket to grab my purse.

"We can sort it out later, don't worry." He flashes me a smile before slipping out of the door and closing it behind him.

With a pair of black leggings, a Bad Wolves t-shirt and

fresh underwear, I lock myself in the bathroom and start shedding my temporary persona so I can get back to being me.

CHAPTER 10

When I come back out of the bathroom dressed, face free of make-up, and a towel wrapped around my wet hair, I'm more comfortable in myself.

Mars has returned and is sitting on the bed with his back propped against the headboard, his legs stretched out in front of him. Although he's positioned at one side of the mattress, he takes up most of the width, and with the generous pile of various snacks at his side, there's not a lot of room, to say the least. No longer is he dressed in a suit but in grey sweatpants and a Capa Cobra's fitted t-shirt. His feet are bare, a pair of Nike trainers and sports socks discarded on the floor. The TV is on, the distinctive noise and sports talk filter into the room. I glance at the screen to see who's playing. While I'm sure that he had been watching the game between the Pittsburgh Steelers and the Cleveland Browns, his eyes are firmly fixed on me.

"What's the score?" I ask in hope that it's enough to direct his attention back to the game and therefore make me feel less conspicuous.

"36-10 to the Browns," he remarks with a deep sigh, clearly not happy at how the game is going.

"No way," I grumble as I climb up onto the other side of the bed so I can get a better view of the TV screen. "What the hell? The Steelers should be handing the Browns their arses." His head snaps around to look at me, his eyebrows almost launching off the top of his head.

"What?" he bellows with amazement. "I thought you said you didn't watch TV, so how…?"

"I stream it on my phone whenever I get the chance," I reply. "Although sometimes the quality's a bit crappy." I pull the towel from my head and start to run my fingers through my hair to try to tame it without the use of a brush.

"I know you come and watch us practice, but I can't believe you're into the NFL."

"You've seen me watching?" This time I'm the one with the amazed expression.

"Sure," he admits, "don't worry, the others haven't seen you. Not yet anyway. So, who's your team? Other than the Capa's of course," he brags giving me a cocky smile. He passes me a chilled bottle of coke from the bedside table.

"The Steelers of course," I gesture to the TV with the bottle in my hand before I screw off the top and take a long swig.

"Jesus, me too," he blurts out making me jump and almost spraying out the mouthful of pop. I swallow and cough a little before turning my gaze to him.

"Favourite player?" I ask keeping the conversation going. I like this surprisingly easy banter that's going on between us and I don't want it to stop.

"Bush, of course," he exclaims with a snigger. That makes sense, seeing as Devin Bush is the inside Linebacker for the Steelers. "What about you?" he counters.

"Harris," I lie because I will not admit that I'm in total agreement with him. Besides, Harris plays offense and not defence like Mars, I mean Bush.

"Yeah, he's good if you're into running backs that is," he teases. "Defence is where it's at though."

"Well, you're bound to say that… Come on ref, are you blind? That was clearly pass interference," I yell at the screen. "Did you see that?" I turn to Mars asking for his opinion.

"Shit, do you know all the rules?" His expression is a mix of gobsmacked and impressed but for some reason, it gets my hackles up.

"Yep, pretty much, as well as rugby, football, hockey. I do draw the line at cricket though. So fucking boring. Why? Do you think because I'm female that I've not got the attributes to do so? Come on Mars, it's 2021 and we have women commentators."

"No, it's just that…"

"It's just what?" I interrupt him because his assumptions of me are pissing me off. "Being a bitchy cheerleader isn't the only requirement you need as a woman to follow sport."

"I'm sorry. I didn't mean it like that. It just surprised me that's all. I didn't have you down as a sports geek."

"No, just a geek and therefore the butt of you and your arsehole friends jokes." I chide back.

"Yeah, about that. Bell is a dick and goes way too far," he admits with a hint of sadness.

"If you think that, then why do you stand there and let

him do it?" I growl back at him. "You never put a stop to it."

"I did," he argues. "And I admit, I shouldn't have waited so long before I spoke up. I should have stood up to him and stopped all this shit months ago." He seems genuinely regretful. Could he be telling me the truth?

"Jesus!" I pant out when it hits me. "It was you in the hallway when Bell was choking me." I gasp as I think back to when Bell had lost it with me and had his hands around my throat. "You're the one that stopped him?"

"God, I'm so sorry," he says moving up and onto his knees to face me. "I'd already told him that the pranking was getting way out of hand, but Bell being Bell, he just laughed it off. The rest of the team were right behind him. I considered putting distance between me and the team, started hanging back, making excuses to be somewhere else other than when we had practice, but then I thought if I was around when he was doing his crazy shit, I could at least keep an eye on him." He drops his head, but when he lifts it back up, his eyes pierce mine, all I see is shame and sincerity in them. "I can't even bear to comprehend what could have happened, how far he would have gone if I hadn't been there to stop him."

I swallow deeply, the intensity of his stare makes me want to reach out to him. But I stop myself.

"I'm so sorry, Hope. It's unforgiveable I know but believe me, I won't ever forgive myself for being part of it."

"I still don't understand," I shake my head at him. "First, despite Bell being your friend you go against him. Then at the school, you step up against my father, to protect me when it could have backfired and got you into so much trouble."

"Still could I suppose if they track us down," he grimaces while running his hand across the back of his neck.

"But why, you don't owe me anything, unless it's your guilt driving you."

"I sure as hell wasn't going to stand there and let your father abuse you like that," he growls, a darkness in his eyes tells me he's pissed. "I know you think I'm an arsehole, but…"

"I don't think you're an arsehole," I interrupt, not sure whether I'd meant to say it out loud rather than keep it in my head. "Not anymore anyway. How could I when you've done all this for me?" I let out a deep, long breath. "I just can't get my head around it. Why the change of heart?"

"Because I fucking like you, okay." He pronounces unexpectedly.

Holy shit. Did I just hear him right? I look at him, really look at him and I see his cheeks are pinked with embarrassment at his outburst.

"I've liked you for what seems like forever," he continues while holding my gaze. "Whenever you're around, I can't help but be drawn to you. Even when you're out of sight, I sense your presence. Not only are you fucking stunning," he says with conviction, "and you don't even realise it. Your determination is immeasurable. The way you took all the teasing, the pranks, all the bullshit, you still showed up at school every day. Not once did you report us to the head, which I wouldn't have blamed you if you had, but instead you continued to brave it out. You are so strong."

"I'm far from strong," I snigger. At this precise moment, I feel anything but because his revelation brings forward my own suppressed feelings for him and it scares me. If I'm honest with myself, Mars was the reason I turned up to watch practice every day. Yes, I like sport, but if it hadn't been for the Capa Cobras Linebacker, a certain Vance Marshall, I'm not one hundred percent sure that I'd have taken such a strong interest in the game.

"I don't mean strong as in lifting 200lbs," he says reaching out and taking my hand in his. "I mean you have an inner strength that is far superior to any other, and that makes you so fucking irresistible that sometimes when I look at you, I can hardly breathe."

"I don't know what to say," I murmur, my heart races at his words and although I should worry that this is just another sick prank set up by Bell, I know by the honesty that is as clear as day on Mars's face, that it isn't.

"And I wouldn't expect you to," he replies with an air of sadness. "Because I've acted like a total dick and you deserve so much better than that." He gives my hand a gentle squeeze before releasing his hold.

"I like you too," I blurt out, snatching his hand back before the warmth of his touch is lost. "Not that I'm sure why I do, but I guess I won't be the first to fall for someone who's been their tormentor."

"Ouch," he smiles softly. "But I guess I deserved that." Mars moves my hand in his so I'm no longer holding his, but he's holding mine and he gives me a gentle tug towards him. I barely keep my balance, almost falling into his lap. "Really, you like me?" he asks, his eyes alight, a cocky grin playing on his lips. "How much?"

"Don't push your luck," I giggle, pushing him in the chest with my free hand. But my laughter is soon snuffed out when he leans forward and covers my mouth with his.

His arm circles around my waist, pulling me all the way into his lap without breaking our kiss.

"Hope," he murmurs against my lips, before kissing me again but this time more forcefully. When I feel his mouth relax, the tip of his tongue pushing forward, I follow his lead and I'm rewarded with a throaty moan of pleasure.

We kiss until we're breathless, our hands explore each other as they slip under fabric until we touch skin. His kiss, his touch is enough to send a million sparks of electricity shooting around my body, the majority congregating between my legs. When his fingertips skim across my hard nipple I gasp at the fire that it ignites in me. My hand slips under the hem of his t-shirt and after I feed my need to graze the firmness of his tight stomach muscles and abs, my hand moves down to the edge of the waistband of his sweatpants.

"No!" Mars halts my hand, bringing it up to his chest. "However much I want you, this isn't the right time. It's too soon."

"You're right," I agree because things are going crazy fast. I go to push away from him but he tightens his hold on me.

"Doesn't mean that I don't want to hold and kiss you," brushing his lips across mine. "Let's talk, there's still a lot about you I don't know."

"I know even less about you," I admit, resting my head against his shoulder.

"Just ask and I'll tell you whatever you want to know," he replies with conviction.

"Do you have brothers, sisters?" I enquire with genuine interest. Sometimes I hate that I'm an only child, but then would I really want a sibling to suffer at the hands of my cruel, oppressive father?

"I have an older sister and brother but they are much older and are living in different parts of the world, so I never see them."

"Don't they visit your parents?" I ask. It's such a shame that he has this family that he doesn't see.

"My parents are rarely at home, so I can't say I blame them. When their own mother and father aren't willing to take a break in their life, why should they?"

"So, you're pretty much left to your own devices?" I reply sadly. "Yet here I am on the other end of the spectrum and almost suffocated by my only living parent."

"I'd rather be in my situation. At least I can come and go as I please. No offence."

"None taken. I agree with you, but it must get lonely at times?"

"Sometimes, but I put all my time into football and the gym anyway, so I can hopefully reach my goal."

"And that is?" I enquire.

"To play in the US NFL of course. Coach says I have potential, and he's going to do everything he can to help me get to where I want to be, to play professionally. But if nothing else, I'm a realist and know that first step is to get accepted into a US college football team and that's one hell of a long shot. It's unlikely to happen." There's a hint of insecurity in his voice so I tilt my head back and look him straight in the eye.

"Don't put yourself down, Mars. You're good enough, in fact you'd be an asset to any team. You have to go for it," I insist. "Because if you don't put everything you have into achieving your dream, then you will end up regretting it further down the line. Don't leave any what-if's lingering in your head, it will just poison your future."

"What do you want, Hope?" His deep, dark eyes are like pools of melted chocolate, not a hint of harshness, just soft and a bit gooey. "Where do you go from here?"

"I have no idea but for now I'd be happy to have my freedom and the chance to make my own choices." I snuggle into his warmth a little more and he moves, taking me with him until we're almost laid flat on the bed.

"You mention that you have an auntie. Why don't you ring her and maybe she could help you?"

"My mum's sister. I barely know her." What I remember from my younger years was that she was my mother's double. I also vaguely remember that when she was due to leave after a visit, I overheard her trying to convince my mother to grab me and anything important to her and go with her. But even though I knew even at that young age that my mother feared my father, she refused. I can't have been the only one that had heard their conversation, because later that day my father lost it and the evidence of his anger marked my mother's skin. I never saw or heard anything of my aunt after that day.

"I don't have her number or even her address." I slap my hand over my mouth as I let out an enormous yawn. I feel the safest and most relaxed I've ever been in Mars's arms and a wave of tiredness suddenly rolls over me. "All I know is her name and that when I last saw her, she lived in the Finchley area of London," I mumble, struggling to keep my eyes open.

"Then I'll help you track her down," he exhales, his hand caressing the back of my head. "It's worth a try. No what-ifs?"

"You don't have to do that; you've already done so much," I say around another yawn.

"Hope, now that I've had the balls to be honest and tell you how I feel about you," He places a gentle kiss on my forehead, "and that you feel it too, I can't walk away from this. No chance in hell."

"Mhm," is all I manage to say before a blanket of sleep takes me under.

CHAPTER 11

I sit on the chair with my back to the desk as I watch a sleeping Mars. His usual hard and serious features, now soft and almost angelic, his dark lashes flutter occasionally while he dreams. Yet he seems to sleep like the dead because when I prised myself from his hold, he didn't budge an inch.

I've been sitting here for at least an hour, my mind working overtime. Options considered. Consequences calculated. Decisions made.

I spin around to face the desk, grab the hotel notepad and pen with a clear and determined mind and I begin to write. Once done, I place the two twenty-pound notes on top and weigh it down with five-pound coins, the rough amount for the room and what he must have spent on snacks from the vending machine.

I pull the backpack onto my back and allow myself to take one last glimpse of beautiful, sleeping Mars. I exhale hard because although my heart aches a little, my head is convinced. I quietly slip out of the room and take my leave.

. . .

Mars,

I'm sorry that I left without saying goodbye, but I couldn't stay however much I wanted to. That wouldn't be right.

My leaving has nothing to do with forgiveness because I do forgive you. How could I not? You saved me and now I'm on the path to freedom. I'm not sure where that path will lead, but I'm going to take it anyway.

You are one special and determined person, Mars, and I don't doubt for one minute that if you put your mind to it, you will achieve your dream. But it's because of that, that I must walk away. I cannot and will not be a distraction that could risk your chance of an amazing future.

Grab every opportunity with both hands, Mars.

No what-ifs. No regrets.

Hope.

CHAPTER 12

"And just when you thought you'd seen the best of this guy. Pow! Marshall surprises us yet again."

"I have to agree with you, Cory."

"Hell, Jeff (laughing) that doesn't happen very often."

"Too true. Too True. This guy always brings his 'A' game on match day. Not only is Vance Marshall one of the highest rated, if not the top, defensive Linebackers of this time, but his adaptability on the field is mind blowing."

"Quite remarkable Jeff, considering the continued news reports about the player."

"Yeah, it's pretty amazing how, despite the bad press coverage and damning photos that have been plastered all over the news, he is the epitome of professionalism when on the field."

"So far, Cory, but I can't help but think that eventually, the bubble is going to burst and the behaviour we're

seeing in his private life is going to bleed over and start to affect his game."

Listening to the game commentators on the radio does nothing to dampen down the nervousness that's been building over the past week. Since I received the news of my temporary position I was about to embark on, I'd had a knot as heavy as a ten-kilo weight sitting in the pit of my stomach.

After flying from London Heathrow to Dallas, the seventeen-hour layover turning into an overnight stay due to a technical fault with the aircraft on my connecting flight to Billings-Logan International airport, I finally got to pick up my rental car; a four door, Chevrolet Malibu in an iridescent pearl colour, and hit the road. All in all, it's been approximately 46 hours since I left my one-bedroomed apartment in Marylebone, and I'm pretty much dead on my feet. All I want to do is crawl into bed, any bed and sleep, but despite the delays in travel and my overwhelming fatigue, I'm expected to turn up to meet the head coach and some of the other coaching squad.

My stomach rolls, nausea threatening in the back of my throat. It's a good thing, because it's the only thing that keeps me from falling asleep at the wheel. Well, that and the utter dread of what kind of reception I'll get.

For the past two years, I've been flitting from one club to another in the U.K. Mainly English football teams, but I have done a couple of Rugby League and Cricket clubs, when they too have run out of options and had to revert to desperate measures.

That's what I am. The last resort.

Because despite the growing need for my particular skills, the sports world is still stuck in the dark ages, much like most of society. The lack of understanding and acknowledgement of mental health issues is still overlooked, and the sporting world is no exception. The stigma of it being a sign of weakness is still profound. But it is improving.

Once the powerheads behind these great sports teams get their heads out of their arses and smell the coffee, that's when I come into my own.

My work has predominately been in the U.K, hence why I'm based in London, but my job has taken me around the country. Liverpool, Manchester, and I've even had to hop the English Channel a couple of times after being seconded to Italian and Spanish clubs, to work with big-name British stars on their payroll.

Most of the time, I'm introduced as a sports psychologist brought in to help specific athletes, but they don't know that I'm not there to help them boost their performance in whatever sport they play. I'm much more than that.

My main field is behavioural psychiatry. So, for all intents and purposes, they think they're seeing someone who will help them up their game. What I'm doing is much deeper than that. I get into their heads, identify their demons, and help to slay them. It increases their dynamics on the field and in their private lives. Although, private is a bit of a joke, as once they hit the sports celebrity status, every move they make, every dubious word that slips from their mouths are there for the paparazzi taking.

Which means I get called in to handle the troubled players. The addicts, the trouble causers and the generally badly behaved. Whether that's butting heads with their managers and coaches or from hitting the headlines. It's generally far from the exemplary role model that they should publicly be for their young fans and followers, therefore putting their sport into disrepute.

This is the first time I've been recruited to work in the U.S.

The first time in the sport that runs in my blood, and that's impregnated in my bones.

American Football.

I finally arrive at the colossal 62,000-seat stadium. The exterior is all silver and glass panels that hide the impressive field behind it, the nucleus of the building. I brought the car to a stop in one of the parking places, as instructed in the email I received before leaving London.

God, I'm dog tired, all I want to do is crawl into the back seat of the car, pull my coat over my head and sleep.

Or am I just trying to delay the inevitable?

I breathe hard through my nose and hold it for five before pushing the air back out between my parted lips. It's the only thing that eases the pending nausea that's lurking in the back of my throat. With the tips of my fingers, I flick down the sun visor, adjusting the mirror until I get the perfect view of my eyes.

I lean further towards the mirror, noticing that my eyes look dry and lacklustre, the whites marbled with red due to lack of sleep. I rummage through my bag until I find the drops that might at least give them some life and a little sparkle. Once administered, the stray fluid dabbed away with the cuff of my hoodie sleeve. I lean back into my seat, but my gaze stays firmly in place.

"Fuck," I curse at my reflection. "Why am I doing this shit?" I take another deep breath before the answer to my question comes clear in my head. Because I couldn't say no to the biggest challenge of my life. My sink or swim moment. "Time to practice what you preach," I whisper under my breath before I lean in close to the mirror again. "I am confident," my stare firm and full of determination. "I have the knowledge and power to succeed. I believe in myself and will achieve my goals." I repeat my mantra a second and third time before I scoop up my bag and step out of the safety of the car with a newfound determination. A quick switch to replace my hoodie with a more professional looking blazer, and I'm locking up and making my way towards the building.

CHAPTER 13

It's been seven years since I'd snuck out of the hotel room, leaving Vance Marshall asleep, and jumped on the first London-bound train. So, seeing Mars after all this time is something I'm kind of dreading.

I won't deny that I'd been riddled with guilt and felt like a first-class ungrateful bitch when I walked away, but I still believe it's what had to be done.

Since then, I'd taken my own route, consuming every inch of knowledge that I could muster throughout my college and university education. While Mars had gained a rare, but not unheard-of, football scholarship to Florida University. Then later went on to sign up with one of the NFL teams. A football club that had evolved from being a low threat, barely scraping into the bottom of the league, to now riding high, right up there with the top five.

So, yeah, the thought of coming face to face with Mars, after all this time was not something I relished. Still, as I'm now walking through the doors of the Montana Longhorns stadium, whose current number one Linebacker is the one and only Vance Marshall, it's only a matter of time before the inevitable happens. Especially as he was top of my hit list of three players that require my expertise.

The automatic doors slide open, and I step inside. Immediately a young, tall, slim woman, who I guess is a similar age to me, with long striking, red hair tied back in a high ponytail, steps forward to greet me. When she gets that bit closer, I can see she has a naturally pretty, makeup-free face and is dressed in black tracksuit pants and a club branded royal blue t-shirt that makes her blue eyes pop.

"Ms. Palmer?" she asks, coming towards me. She doesn't offer a hand in greeting as they are firmly locked behind her back, and the wavering smile on her face tells me that she's nervous.

"Yes," I respond, and just out of pure devilment, I hold out my hand to shake. "And you are?"

"Oh, erm… Lucy, ma'am. Lucy Williams." She wipes her hand down the leg of her pants before taking hold of mine. Her handshake is soft and unsure, so I give her hand a friendly squeeze before letting go.

"Well, Lucy. Can you do me one thing?" I smile at her, taking in her wide eyes and partly open mouth as a clear sign that she's taken aback by my relaxed demeanour. "Please call me Hope, and less of the Ma'am. It kind of makes me feel like I'm royalty or something."

Her hand comes up to her mouth as she tries to hide her giggles. "I'll try to remember," she exclaims once she regains composure. "But you do kind of sound like the… "

"Don't tell me," I sigh, holding up my hand and in a light-hearted way saying, "I sound like the Queen." I snigger. "Believe me, my northern accent, which I'm proud that I've retained despite of living in the south of England for the past few years, is nothing like English aristocracy."

"I'm sorry. I didn't mean to insult you in any way," Lucy quickly chirps up.

"Oh, I know, and it's all good." I reassure her. "Now, I guess you're here to take me to meet Coach Scully, so why don't you lead the way?"

"Yes. Sorry," Lucy gushes. "I'm…" I hold up my hand to her, and halt her from apologising yet again. She looks at me with wide eyes before dropping her gaze to the floor. I visibly see her take a deep breath, roll her shoulders, then lift her head high. A big, closed smile plastered on her face. "If you'd like to follow me Ms… Hope, I'll take you to the locker room."

Locker room! Holy fuck.

Thank God the place is at the other end of the building because it gives me time to repeat my mantra in my head. There is something about an all-male locker room that gets my heart pumping. It's all that manliness, testosterone, and natural body odour. It makes me a little lightheaded and a lot turned on.

Damn it! Over the years, I've tried to avoid the place, especially on training and game days, preferring to see the players in the gym, or when on a one-on-one basis, in an office or treatment room.

A flash of a memory from my school days jumps into my head. The sneaking into the locker room to prank certain team members, the FUB's to be exact. I'll never forget the Nutella pants.

I was expecting my introduction to the coaches and a handful of the training squad to be held in one of the conference rooms, but I guess the location is irrelevant. When I get nearer to where I assume we are heading, it becomes obvious that my idea of a small and unassuming welcoming committee is way off the mark.

A deep, robust voice bellows out from the already open doors, and it's blatantly obvious from the loud and dominating way he's talking that there's more than a handful of people in there.

When I step up to the doorway and peek inside, I gulp at the sight. The room is huge but doesn't seem it because it's wall-to-wall with players. Some sit in their designated changing area, some stand or hunker down in the centre of the room. Every single person's attention is solely on the big bear of a man with a bald head, round kind face, with a white goatee beard, standing dead centre in the room.

It looks like they've just finished a training session due to the kit they're wearing. Or should I say part wearing as the majority are minus their shirts. The sight of a handful of them still wearing their shoulder pads sends a shudder through me from my head to my toes at the realisation I'm here and this is actually happening.

It looks like the whole squad is in the room. Fifty-three to be exact, going by the stats that I'd swotted up on before I came. That's not including the coaches, physio's, etcetera that seem to be in here too.

I know most of them, although some of their profile pictures are obviously outdated. But Coach Scully is easy to identify as I've seen him on the screen while catching the odd game.

Who am I trying to kid? I watch every single game even if it's by means of catch-up.

"Now, lay your hand on the shoulder of the player at your side," Coach instructs his team, and immediately they follow suit. "We are one team, one dream and will fight to win. Better tomorrows come from hard work today. Always earned, never taken for granted." The room vibrates with the words that every single person in the room chants. Not one person doesn't follow, showing great respect for their main man. I'm engrossed in the sight and the deep hum of the collective voices that I miss some of what has been said, but pick it up again when Coach booms out, "Work. Hard." The room explodes with a noisy 'Hit. Hard,' response. "Play. Hard." Coach bellows out even louder which is met with a 'Win. Easy.' "And why is that?" Coach lifts his hand, his finger pointing as he does a 360 turn where he stands, making sure he points to every single player. Silence hits the room, but only for a matter of seconds before it erupts with an ear bursting. "Because that's how we roll."

I stand and watch while they move around each other, offering hugs, high fives and some even going in for a playful tackle. Based on what I've witnessed just now, it's clear that one thing is for sure. The Montana Longhorns is collectively a strong team, with each and every one of the players and management holding great respect for their fellow members.

"Hold up," Coach shouts once the rowdiness has dampened down. "Just one more thing before you head into the showers." The burly man cuts through the crowd, making a beeline towards me. I'd been so distracted that I hadn't even realised he'd noticed my arrival. A big smile adorned his face, in total contrast to the authoritative persona I'd just observed. It has an instant calming effect on me, and I find myself smiling right back.

Once he gets to my side, without saying a word, he

wraps his big arm around my shoulder and leads me back to where he was originally standing.

"We have a new member of the team, albeit temporary. Gentlemen, this young lady here is Ms. Palmer, and she will be with us for the next three months." The air rumbles with greetings, but it's a mix of positivity and negativity.

"What's she doing here?" A deep growl of a voice barks out above the crowd, the question thick with hostility.

"I beg your pardon?" Coach snaps back, with equal sharpness, turning in the direction of where the voice has come from. I follow his movement, but I know without even looking for confirmation exactly who's behind the animosity.

I'd felt his presence as soon as I'd got inside the room.

CHAPTER 14

Like some kind of sexy arse, NFL God with his blond hair and Nordic vibe, Vance Marshall parts the waves of heavenly teammates, coming forward until he's standing a few feet in front of us. When he speaks, his attention is purely on Coach when he adds in a much more hospitable tone, "Sorry, Coach. What I meant to say is, why is Ms. Palmer here?"

"Hope, is here to work with you guys to help you all up your game."

"With all due respect, Coach. The staff we have in place are already doing a more than adequate job. The stats are clear for all to see, so I can't honestly think that Ms. Palmer...," his attention flicks to me, but it's fleeting, not giving me a chance to get a fair evaluation of his feelings, but there's a distinct air of disdain. "...has anything of any benefit to us."

"Well, Marshall, what the management says goes, and as they're paying good money for Ms. Palmer to be here, then they obviously think she does," Coach replies, loud enough so the rest of the room can hear. "So, I expect you all to get with the program and treat Hope here with nothing but the greatest respect." I sense my cheeks heating as all eyes fall on me. Most of them give me varying levels of a smile, some a curt but acceptant nod. "Now hit the showers."

As they all start to move around the room, I stay beside Coach, waiting for him to give me some kind of direction on what to do now.

"Marshall!" he suddenly yells, making me jump out of my skin. Damn, this place makes me nervous. Or is it just a certain 6'1 linebacker that's got me so jittery? "When you've done with your shower, I want to see you in my office."

Mars turns his head, glancing over his shirt covered muscular shoulder. "Yes, Coach," he replies, pushing the words through his clenched teeth. His eyes clash with mine, and even though he's a good few feet away, I see the same darkness in his eyes. The same darkness that I remember from my school years when he was one of my tormentors. I thought we'd got past that. I thought that we were on a different level. But by the way he looks at me, even for mere seconds, I can tell that he's pissed. Holy fucking shit, is he pissed, and not for one minute do I think that it's directed at anyone else other than me.

"Come on, Hope," Coach gently tugs on my arm, making me snap my eyes away from Mars' retreating form. "Let me show you to the room we have all set up for you."

"Bit of a frosty welcome, I got there," I joke nervously as we walk down the hallway towards a bank of lifts.

"Don't worry about that lot. They'll soon cowboy up." Leaning forward, Coach Scully pushes at all the call buttons, each one lighting up red as he hits them. On the fourth button, a set of doors open instantaneously.

"Cowboy up?" I ask curiously as we step into the lift.

"They'll deal with it, accept it. Most of them you won't have any trouble with, but those you do, then you come straight to me."

"Let me guess. They'll be the ones that need the additional sessions?" I huff out. "Not sure what you can do if they simply refuse to work with me."

"Believe me, every single one of our players live to play, so all I need to do is threaten to bench them and it'll soon get them in line." The lift doors open, and we step out into a long, narrow hallway banked at one side with window views of the Montana skyline. The other, a selection of solid wood doors with various nameplates on them.

"For a minute there, I was wondering what kind of punishment you were going to use as leverage," I snigger.

"Oh, sweet girl. Don't think for one minute that if it came to it, I wouldn't butt kick any of those hammer heads if they stepped out of line and disrespected a lady."

"Hey, Coach," I laugh out loud, louder than I intended to. Then I start to babble. "I hate to crush your impression of me, but it won't take long, when you hear my cursing and such, that you'll quickly realise I'm far from a lady."

Yes, I get nervous whenever I start a new position, but this isn't my first rodeo. I've worked with some of the biggest football (or should I start calling it soccer while I'm here?) teams, but this is surreal. Maybe it's because I'm now in the U.S. Or maybe it's due to the fact that for the first time in my life I'm living the dream. My dream. The sport that runs through my veins, gets my heart pumping and is prominent in my private life, has now, at last, merged with my work life. This could be the pinnacle of my career or the start of so much more.

"A little cursing? You haven't heard me yet." He comes to a stop in front of one of the doors. The silver, shiny name plaque fixed to the front of this one has my knees almost buckling. Hope Palmer is in big, black capital letters for all the world to see. "Hope, I think you and I will get on just fine."

When he pushes open the door and I step inside, I'm blown away. The room is large and airy. One side has an adjustable bed and other equipment, which will be perfect for the physical side of my job, like muscle manipulation, massage and such. Yes, I do that too. It's all part of the package, and I'm multi-faceted. The other side of the room is in total contrast. It could be mistaken for any living room in a middle-class house. It holds a couch, coffee table, and a couple of high back armchairs. One wall is covered by a single large unit that has shelves, cupboards, and a flat-screen T.V. But what really makes this room, the thing that makes my heart rate tachycardic, is the floor to ceiling glass that faces out onto the stadium ground. When I walk over to the window, I'm mesmerized by the stark white markings against the rich green of the field. The sky is a perfect powder blue and the sun beating down gives the whole place a heavenly glow.

"Pretty special, isn't it?" Coach softly says when he comes and stands beside me. "I never get bored with it."

"That sure is one fucking amazing view," I pant out. "I'll take this over a picturesque sunset any day."

"Now I know we're going to get on," Coach chuckles. "Why don't you take a look around? You should find everything you asked for in the cabinets, but if we've missed anything we can get it ordered through the front office." He says as he walks back over to the door. Turning back around to face me, he adds. "Make a list, and then when you're ready, come find me in my office. It's the last door down the hall, then we can talk further."

"Sounds good." I smile and continue to watch until he steps back into the hallway and closes the door behind him. Now on my own, I let out a mouth wide, face scrunching, silent scream while bouncing on my feet. This is far more than I ever could have imagined, and my life has just got mind-blowingly crazy and oh so fucking good.

CHAPTER 15

After checking out everything in the room, I slip back into the hallway. I'm on a super high, almost skipping my way to Coach's office. A quick knock on the door, still riding on this amazing buzz, I push open the door with a flurry and step into the office. "I think I have everything I need except…" When I glance up from the shortlist that I'd made on my iPhone notes app, my euphoria is instantly quashed when both Coach and Mars's head swings in my direction. They're standing face to face in the centre of the room, and even to the untrained eye, it's clear that they're in the middle of a heated dispute.

"Sorry, you're busy," I blurt out, suddenly feeling considerably awkward. Fuck, I'd forgotten that Coach had instructed his top linebacker to also come to his office. I should have held back, at least until I'd known the coast was clear. This only becomes clearer when I catch sight of the contempt in Mars' dark eyes as he takes me in. His gaze seems to seep through the skin of my face like acid. "I'll come back later," I exhale quickly. I spin around and grab the door handle, ready to make a speedy exit, only to be stopped in my tracks by Coach's deep, baritone voice.

"Not necessary. I need to talk to you both together, anyway."

"I get it," Mars barks out before Coach gets a chance to speak further. "She's here to help the team heighten their skills. So, shouldn't you be telling them that? I'm already at the top of my game and not in need of any mind over matter, psychobabble. Roster it up for those who need it." Before I know it, he's pushing past me to get to the door that I'm still hovering near, not sure of what to do. His shoulder brushes mine, and the static electricity that jumps between us crackles audibly.

"Get the fuck back here, Marshall. This meeting isn't over until I say it is."

Mars' back becomes rigid with anger as he turns to face Coach again. His eyes connect with mine and are still seeped with the same hatred that I saw in the locker room and when I first walked into this office. "Coach," he hisses between gritted teeth.

"Shut up and sit-down Marshall, before you push me too far and force me to bench your cranky ass." The air is thick with tension, and I can tell by Mars' body language that he's teetering on the edge. Whether to do as Coach ordered or tell him to go fuck himself.

I really don't like how this is going, and the last thing I want is for these two to butt heads because of my secondment within the team. This has to work. I need it to work because otherwise, what the hell am I doing here?

There's no denying that seeing Mars has affected me more than I thought it would after all this time. I never expected us to react like two long-lost friends, but the level of his negativity towards me has knocked the wind out of me, along with my tenacity. But it's time I pushed all that aside. If he wants to be the arsehole, the FUB of old, then bring it on. I, will be nothing but the professional that my five years of intense education and bloody hard work have led me to.

With my back straight, my arms firmly by my side, I stride confidently over to one of the two armchairs placed at this side of a deep mahogany desk that's littered with various papers and sports paraphernalia. There's a silver picture frame resting on one side of the desk with its back towards me, and despite being tempted to reach for it so I can see what's on the flip side, I resist. No doubt it's a family photo because I do know one thing about Coach, and that is that he's a wife, two kids and a dog kind of family man. Instead, I sit, fold one leg over the over and rest my forearms across the arms of the chair. I can feel Mars' eyes on me, so I meet them, my gaze then quickly flicking to the other vacant chair. It's a subtle move but nonetheless a challenge for him to take a seat. I watch his brows pinch together, a clear sign that my actions are confusing to him. He'll get it, eventually.

I'm not the weak Hope 'hopeless' Palmer, that he undoubtedly remembers back in school. Well, I guess that's his impression with the caustic way he's reacting towards me.

It's not until Coach walks around to the far side of his desk and slides into the black, high-backed executive chair that Mars makes his move and reluctantly drops into the remaining seat.

"There's no point beating about the bush with this Marshall, so I'm just going to come right out and say it." Couch leans back in his chair, his face as straight as a plank of wood. "The board are concerned about your behaviour…"

"My behaviour? Are you sure they're not getting me mixed up with Marsden? He's the one who's getting flagged in nearly every game," he says defensively. "I've not received one this season."

"I'm not talking about the game, son. I'm talking about off the field," Coach leans forward on the desk, resting his elbows on top of a copy of Gridiron, Pro Football and I'm sure I see the top of a copy of USA Today sports weekly magazines too. "You've been hitting the headlines, Marshall, and not always for the right reasons."

"My private life is my business," he bites back.

"Not when it's plastered on the front page of every sports magazine, not just in America but across the fucking globe." He picks up one of the magazines and throws it in his direction.

Mars scarcely blinks when it comes towards him, catching it before it hits him in the face. He holds it between his hands, and glances down at the copy of The National Enquirer. His left brow rises, and a smirk plays across his full lips, but he doesn't say a word.

"May I?" I ask, leaning over to take it from his hand. He's unwilling to let go at first, but I tug harder until he releases it. He scowls at me as I sit back and stare down at the front page. I glance back up to find that annoying smirk is back on his face. I know that he's expecting me to react to the picture of him, obviously drunk out of his head and misbehaving.

He's shirtless, and the photographer has got the light perfectly right to show the definition of the taut muscles of his chest. Not so much for the dark-haired bimbo that's laid across his lap wearing a bright pink mini-skirt and matching hooker heels. Her fake tits are out for all to see, only her pixilated nipples giving a minuscule amount of coverage. But what stands out the most due to the big red arrow pointing it out, not that it isn't already obvious enough, is Mars' hand buried high up between her parted legs. With an expression of pure rapture on her face, there's no doubt that he's hit her sweet spot.

He doesn't realise that I've already seen this, plus the majority of all the other images snapped by the paps of him caught in compromising positions, with numerous different women. So, if he expects to see a shocked expression on my face, he's going to be greatly disappointed.

"Not the best impression to give to all your young fans, Vance," I say with an even tone to my voice. "It is okay to call you Vance, isn't it?" I don't give him a chance to answer. "Although I have seen worse. Caught with your pants down, bare arse showing while being blown by the wife of the front man of the TV show you'd just been interviewed on, now that was below the belt, no pun intended."

His face to anyone else would be void of any expression, because the signs are so subtle that to the untrained eye it would be difficult to detect, but for me, it's as obvious as traffic lights. The instant dilation of his pupils that, of course, can suggest a multitude of emotions. The barely visible tick of the muscle just below his ear, also tells me he's trying his best not to clench his jaw too hard. It's enough for me to conclude that he's as angry as a bear who can't find a wood to shit in. He opens his mouth to say something but snaps it back shut when Coach slaps the flat of his palm on the desk, causing the papers to lift and scatter even further. A couple of them fall to the floor, but he ignores them.

"Exactly, Marshall. You need to clean up son, because it's starting to have a negative effect on the sport."

"But not my game," Mars bellows out, his temper starting to show its ugly face. "As long as I excel on the field, who gives a toss?"

"The parents of the fourteen-year-old who lives and breathes football and all that is Vance Marshall, Linebacker for the Montana Longhorns, that's who." I counter before Coach gets the chance. "Do you seriously think that they want him to grow up thinking that it's okay to drink yourself into oblivion and act like a narcissistic arsehole, with no respect for women or relationships, for that matter?"

"I'm not narcissistic," The tick and tightness of his jaw are now prominent, but the deep growl of his voice alone is enough that even a blind man could pick-up on how utterly pissed he is. I suppress the shudder that his tone ignites because the last thing I want is for him to see that he's affecting me. If he thinks he's got the upper hand, I might as well grab my bags and take my arse back to the airport. "Besides, if the parents are stupid enough to let their kids read that trash, then it's their own stupid fault."

"That's a textbook response. Deflecting," I tut, shaking my head. Totally patronizing, but hell, the way he's acting is verging on a petulant child.

"Damn it, son. It's time you take responsibility for your actions," Coach speaks up.

"And what if I don't?" Mars smirks, his cocky attitude bubbling to the surface.

Coach shoots out of his chair, slamming his hands to the surface of the desk. He leans forward, bracing himself with his outstretched arms. "If you think you're indispensable, you're mistaken. In fact, the board has made it clear that they will no longer tolerate this level of disrespectful, shameless conduct on or off the field. As far as they're concerned, you have become too much of a liability and if you don't clean up your act, then your contact with the club will be suspended."

"They can't do that," Mars grits out as he jumps to his feet. "They wouldn't do that."

"Well, they won't if you stop being a total prick and take the help that they're offering you."

"What help, her?" He swings me a dark and cutting glare. "A sports psychologist?" he spits.

"And behavioural psychiatrist." Bugger me! Mars has changed from the expressionless eighteen-year-old I remember from before. Or am I a damn sight better at reading people now? Guess my five years of intense university education was worthwhile, even if only to get a read on my old school nemesis.

But he wasn't your enemy when you last saw him, now was he?

He helped you get away from a volatile situation, then opened up to you and told you how he felt.

He kissed you like he wanted you, like the air he breathed.

He had shown you real emotion, offered to help you escape your life.

Then, like a coward, you walked away.

"You ungrateful asshole," Coach hisses, bringing Mars' attention away from me and back to him. "The board has employed Ms. Palmer, Hope, predominantly for your benefit and because she is the best in her field, so I will not have you undermining her in any way."

"But you don't understand. I know her."

"I know that. So, what if you both went to the same high school over seven years ago, back in England?" Wow, I didn't realize Coach was aware of that but it looks like he doesn't care. "That's a lot of water under the bridge. Unless there's something you need to tell me about, like you two were boyfriend and girlfriend or something?"

"Fuck, no." Mars scowls, shouting out far too quickly. "We weren't even friends." He adds with equal venom and hits me with a dark, dismissive glare. I realise hurts me more than it should, when a sharp pain hits my chest, dead centre.

"Then suck it up, buttercup. You'll be involved in the team sessions along with three or four one-on-one sessions with her every week. End of discussion."

CHAPTER 16

It's now Wednesday, four days since I touched down in Montana. Maybe touched down isn't the right word to use, but it does sort of go with the whole football scenario. Coach decided that I needed a few days to get settled into the accommodation that I'll be calling home for the next few months. Also, time to let the jet lag run its course, telling me that I wasn't expected to officially start at the club until Saturday. I, however, am already going stir crazy and want to get down to business. By the end of the day I'd arrived, I'd unpack my two suitcases and given the two bedroomed place a once over. It hadn't taken long, seeing how cleaners had already been in to take care of everything in lieu of my pending arrival.

I'd expected to stay in a hotel room during my time here but it turns out that wasn't the case. After following the directions I'd been given, I was surprised, to say the least, when I arrived outside a very stylish block of condos. Sizeable windows and large balconies were dominant amongst the brick and white rendered exterior. It was difficult to figure out where one apartment stopped and another began, which gave you a false impression of how generous they were inside. Because when I took the lift to the top floor, punched in the security code to open the door and stepped inside, the breath I took in sharply got well and truly stuck in my throat.

The high ceilings, the abundance of light through the large windows, the clean, crisp lines of the open plan living and kitchen area are showroom stunning. The bloody kitchen itself, with its white, high gloss doors, stainless steel and black granite worktop, was bigger than my whole apartment at home. The living area, complete with two large white fabric sofas placed in an L shape, a black wood table separating them, sat next to an open fireplace. The impressive black painted chimney breast reached up to the super high ceiling. The plush rug on the hardwood floor and abstract artwork tying in perfectly with the colour scheme, finished the look. It's homely, yet modern and fucking breathtakingly lush.

I'd cracked out a 'Jesus H Christ' when I'd flipped open a couple of the kitchen cupboards to find that it was fully stocked with everything I'd need. The big American fridge freezer hiding behind another glossy door was fully stocked, too. Damn, there's even a chilled drinks fridge with beer, vodka, every shade of wine and champagne, which made me laugh out loud as I wondered if this was normal in Montana, or if they'd been influenced by the inflated tales of the English and their drinking habits. It wasn't until after checking the large outside terrace with heart-stopping views across a lake that, when stepping back inside, I noticed the upper floor. The second bedroom was on the same floor, but a set of spiral stairs took you to an open walkway shrouded with more floor to ceiling glass towards a short hallway. The master bedroom and en-suite bathroom impressive, with a shower so high-tech that I might need to take a master's degree on how to use it. There's lots of closet space and a bed big enough for a foursome, if I ever happened to fulfil my fantasy. Finishing off this exquisite accommodation is a house bathroom with double sinks, shower cubical and a free-standing bath that with my short-arseness, would need some serious negotiation when it comes to getting in and out of it.

I spent day two checking out the area and picking up a few things, such as favoured toiletries, fresh fruit and vegetables for my morning smoothies. Day three, after a few hours in the onsite gym that I happened to fall upon, I had vegged out on the sofa with a bucket load of popcorn and binge watched the fourth series of Chicago Fire for the third time. Yep, I could have paid for series five and six, but hey, it goes against my Yorkshire blood to pay for something that will probably be free in a couple of months. I decided that however much I loved my new living environment, enough was enough. Today, day four, I made my way into the club.

When I walk into my office, I get another rush of 'I can't quite believe that this is my life' buzz. In my arms, I have a box of massage oils that I swear by, and the hand-held recording machine that I use. I write notes too, but I'm always a little paranoid that I might miss something, a gasp, a waver in their voice or simply the tone. I find it comes in very handy when I'm putting all my information onto my database. I'm just placing the last bottle of oil onto the shelf near the massage table when there's a knock on the door.

"Come on in," I shout, wondering who has noticed me slip in, even though I haven't passed anyone on the way.

"Hey," Lucy's head appears from around the partially open door. "I thought I saw your car in the parking lot."

"Morning Lucy." I hand gesture for her to come into the room. "What can I do for you?"

"I..." she stammers as she steps up to the other side of my desk. "I'm so sorry, I wasn't expecting you in until Saturday, so I wasn't prepared."

"Prepared for what?" I question, not sure why she's being so apologetic.

"To have your schedule ready for you so I could make any amendments. And anything else you might need, of course," she replies. The bridge of her nose and forehead creases as she looks back at me. "As your assistant?"

"Assistant?" I snigger. "I didn't even know I had one. Tell me, Lucy, what actually is your job role here at the club?"

"I'm meant to be the assistant to the coaches, and now of course you, but as the teams PR manager walked out a little over a week ago, I've been asked to cover the role as much as I can until they can recruit someone new."

"That's some expensive, high-level shoes you're having to fill."

"It's only for a little while," she says to justify the situation. "So, if you don't mind me asking, why are you here?"

"Watching Kelly Severide was getting me far too hot and frisky. I nearly got out my toy box," I let out a long, dramatic sigh while fluttering my eyelashes.

"Really?" she giggled behind her hand. "Funny, he has the same effect on me."

We both laugh out loud, and I get the sense that Lucy could quite possibly be my bestie while I'm here, because by the looks of it, the female species within the club is limited.

"Anyway," she says when we both stop acting silly. "I have the first few appointments set-up for you and also player files." She drops a handful of grey cardboard folders onto my desk.

"Jesus, don't they believe in interface technology in this place?" I gasp, astounded that they were still working on paper.

"Some don't," she chuckles. "But not to worry, it's all on the database too, it's just I wasn't sure if like some of the coaches, you prefer the less," she air quotes "technical option." Flipping the top folder in front of me open, she points to the first page. "Your personal login and password to get on the main system are here. But there's also information on how to set up your own secure folder, how to password protect and secure it to stop anyone else from seeing your notes and records. Even coach Scully won't have access. This is purely for your access only. I know it goes without saying that we recommend you change your passwords on a regular basis and never share with anyone."

"Of course, and I believe despite the fact that I stick strictly to the patient confidentiality rule, that I'll be required to sign a non-disclosure agreement for each of the players I work with on a one-to-one basis."

"Yes, I'm sorry, but the players are insisting on it."

"You mean Vance Marshall is insisting on it?" This is going to be fun… Not!

"There's a brand-new laptop, which has already been setup and checked by our IT department, in the bottom drawer of your desk," Lucy replies, giving me the distinct impression that she's not comfortable responding to my comment.

Avoid. Avoid. Avoid.

"A desktop, monitor, keyboard and mouse are due to be installed on Friday, but I'll get IT to get it done today."

"That would be great. So, when is my first victim due to be hauled into my den of psychological horror?" I ask her with a straight face.

"Monday," Her face is serious, but suddenly her eyes light up when she realises I'm just messing with her. "Shit." Her hand immediately comes to cover her mouth before it opens as she laughs out. "You're going to make coming to work a whole lot better."

"What are you doing tonight?" I ask her out of the blue.

"Nothing, why?"

"Do you fancy showing me where is good around here to get a drink?" I ask hopefully, as the last thing I want to do is spend another night in doing jack-shit.

"No, sorry," Lucy replies, her head cocked to one side. "But I can show you GREAT places around here to grab a drink." She teases, and I quickly catch a glimpse of her perfect smile before once again her hand falls over her mouth.

I can only assume that at some point, Lucy has had braces or some kind of mouth issue and has been ridiculed or embarrassed about it. From that, her mouth covering when she smiles has become somewhat of a habit. Because from what I have seen when she smiles, it is dazzling and certainly shouldn't be covered up.

CHAPTER 17

As it turns out, Lucy has a one bed apartment right near where she's planning on taking me. So, around eight-thirty, after we'd both had time to get back to our respective homes, shower and change, Lucy pulls up outside my condo block. After getting a general rundown of what kind of bar we're going to tonight, I plump for a pair of black fitted jeans that make my arse look incredible and an oversized off the shoulder, lightweight jumper in cobalt blue. It's big and baggy, making most people think I'm trying to hide my body shape. In fact, my boobs are an ample handful if you have big hands, my waist nips in pretty tight and with the work that I do put in at the gym (well, I could hardly tell my clients to push themselves to the limit if I didn't sing from the same hymn sheet) my hips and arse have just the right curviness to make me feel good about my figure. I'm a dress for comfort kind of girl, rather than wearing something so restraining that you end up walking like a robot. The strap of a small bag, that's just big enough for my bank card, phone, a few dollars in cash and a nude lipstick, is slung across my body.

Apparently, the locals only dress to the max if they're going to high-end events, weddings and the like, or maybe one of the two night clubs that are further out of town. When I get a look at Lucy's outfit, which is similar jeans, bright orange halter neck top and leather jacket, I'm confident that I've made a stellar choice. The flat boots I'm wearing are a no-brainer as Lucy has already explained that once we drop her car back at her apartment, we will have a bit of a walk until we hit the first bar.

Despite the heat of the day, the evening is pretty chilly, but I'm not worried that I don't have a coat because we British girls are used to going out with only limited clothing in the perishingly cold English weather.

We've not long since arrived at the first drinking hole, a sports bar called 'Time Out', and I take a seat at the only available booth while Lucy grabs our drinks from the bar opposite. The place is buzzing, the atmosphere electric. Large flat screen T.V's sit at all four corners of the room, currently showing a baseball game between the Tigers and the White Sox. Sports memorabilia of all kinds fill every available space on the walls and ceilings. Even the bathroom signs have been fashioned from the front sections of a football helmet.

"This place is amazing," I tell Lucy as she sucks vodka and cranberry through a straw from a highball glass. "I'm loving the vibe."

"Yeah, it's pretty cool here and popular," she gestures to the high number of people around us. "We're lucky to get a seat." The rest of the booths are crammed. Hip to Hip. Elbow to Elbow.

"It's busy, that's for sure."

"If you think this is busy, you should see it on a weekend. You can barely move in here for all the hot sports jocks."

"Ha, so this is the place to be if you're looking to snag yourself a rich or up-and-coming sports star?"

"You could say that," her eyes lazily work their way around the room before they fall back on me. I smirk at her. "Not that I'm looking for that," she gushes with wide eyes. "I'm comfortable here, even if I come on my own because I know a lot of them. It doesn't matter what sport you play, they all get along, and that's nice."

"Have you always lived around here, Lucy?" I probe, wanting to know more about her.

"This is my hometown, but I spent a few years over in D.C, while completing my education."

"So, how come you've got lumbered with all this extra PR work, can't one of the club managers take that on until they get a new person?" From what I've seen, Lucy is more than capable as a personal assistant, but being the PR for the Club is totally different ball game. "That's some difficult shoes to fill."

"I guess because it was my major at Washington University, they thought I'd be capable of covering for a few weeks," She shrugs her shoulders like it's no big deal.

"You have a PR & Strategic Coms degree?" My eyes bug out because I'll be honest, that kind of surprises me. No wonder the Club has pushed the extra work her way. I bet they're not paying her dues though.

"Masters actually, GPA of 3.79," she says proudly.

"I have no idea what that means but I guess by the look on your face that it's a good grade?"

"It's a fucking phenomenal grade, but when I apply for jobs and they see that I'm only twenty-six, I don't hear back," she sighs, her shoulders drop making me think that she's already feels defeated.

"I get you," I reply sympathetically, because I do. "It wasn't easy for me to get taken seriously at the beginning. It's the typical chicken and egg situation. They will only overlook your young age if you have the experience to back up your credentials, but you can't get the experience if they don't ignore the age thing and give you a chance. I've been there. I'm only 25 myself."

"So, how did you get where you are now?" she rests her elbows and leans in further towards me from the other side of the table, waiting on my big secret.

"I begged, pleaded and worked for free." I breath out heavily. Saying out loud has me realising how ridiculous that sounds.

"You didn't get paid?" she scolds. "Isn't that financial suicide?"

"Oh, it might have seemed that way at first. They thought I was crazy. But I made it clear that after three months, that they had to give me an honest and detailed reference for the work and improvements that I made while there."

"You were that confident?" she gasps.

"Not really, but it was my one chance of getting my foot on the ladder, so I put everything I had into it." I drain the rest of the pink gin from my glass. I slide to the edge of the bench seat to go get us another round.

"Wait," Lucy stops me before I get to my feet. "Did they stick to the agreement?"

"It was irrelevant really, because after six weeks they offered me a job." Stepping away from the table, I move over to order and squeeze my way in between the crowd of people standing around.

"Same again?" the bartender asks, and I'll admit with the amount of people here, remembering what people have ordered previously is a sign of good staff.

"Yes please," I reply with a smile.

"Really sorry, but…" he cringe smiles at me, "I'm going to have to ask you for I.D."

"Oh, shit. Yeah," I stammer as I zip open the back pocket of my bag and pull out my driving license.

"English," The blond-haired server, smirks back at me when he's checked out the details of the card. His eyes are the bluest of blues, his square jaw covered with a perfectly trimmed stubble that works perfectly with his dusky pink lips and slightly crooked nose. All in all, very pleasing to the eye. "You royalty? Because you sure do sound like it." Oh hell. Here we go again. Normally such a stupid comment would put me off, but he is kind of pretty to look at, so I decide, what the hell, let's have some fun instead.

"Cor blimey governor," I reply with my best cockney accent. "Would you Adam and Eve it. How'd you guess?" I quickly look from side to side before leaning in, to which the bartender moves in closer. I get a subtle burst of his woody cologne and lemon zest. "I'm the illegitimate daughter of the second duke of Westyorkchester but I'd rather you kept schtum, because I'm staying here on my jack jones, and I don't want any barney rubble."

"What?" He blurts out, his eyebrows meeting in the middle of his forehead as his mouth drops open, giving me a flash of a silver ball piercing in the middle of his tongue.

Nice.

I can't help it. I just burst into a fit of laughter. "I'm joking. Yes, I'm English but I'm as related to the queen as you are to Donald Trump."

"Actually, he's my uncle," he replies stoically.

"STOP!" Heat comes to my face. Shit, he is blond and tanned but is far removed from the man who waves to his adoring fans with his hair.

"Gotcha!" he laughs, holding out my I.D. towards me, that's slipped between his index and middle finger. I go to take it, but he doesn't let go. "By the way, happy birthday. I better get you your drinks."

"It's on me, seeing as today is a special day," he offers when I go to pay.

"That's really nice of you but let me at least pay from my friend's drink."

"I couldn't have that now, could I?" he winks. "Otherwise, you wouldn't be obliged to return the offer of buying me one back sometime, would you?" Was that a roundabout way of asking to meet up? Before I get a chance to ask, he's moved further down the bar and started taking an order from another customer. He casts me a quick yet generous smile, before grabbing a couple of glasses and turning towards the optics. I take that as my cue to go back to the table and Lucy.

The body count in here seems to have tripled in the few minutes that I was at the bar, and the area is crowded as people hustle to get served. Which makes it difficult when trying to make my way back to Lucy. I sidestep and twist, trying not to spill anything on myself or anyone else as I negotiate my way back. Eventually, I break through the crowd only to find that Lucy is no longer on her own.

"Marshall," I say in greeting while placing our drinks on the table. I slide back onto the seat opposite, where he sits up close to Lucy. The black short-sleeved t-shirt he's wearing fits tight across his chest, and for a moment, I let my eyes linger there. He's always had a great physique, but the additional years since I last saw him and his undisputed dedication to his sport have definitely enhanced it. His body fills out most of the booth, and his posture is relaxed with his arm resting across the back of the seat behind Lucy. His hand dropped, cupping her shoulder, his fingers slowly stroking and caressing her bare skin. With every flex, the cuff of the cotton around his bicep is stretched to the max, the ink on his skin dancing. I'd like to ignore the pang of annoyance that hits me, but damn there's no denying it. You see, in my opinion, he's far too close to her, far too handsy and it's simply not acceptable when he's meant to be cleaning up his act.

"Hopeless," he sniggers, using the name that I thought I'd left behind in youth. "What brings you here? I wouldn't have thought that this was your scene."

"It's a sports bar. What's not to like?"

"You know, the fact that it's full of people, having fun and socialising. From what I can remember you were a bit of a social misfit." Obviously, he's trying to get a rise out of me, but hell, I'm not that girl anymore.

"Wait!" Lucy interjects. "You two know each other?"

Instead of responding to her, I decide to avoid as I'm not sure how much of my past I want to rake up. So, I hit back at him instead.

"You should know better than anyone, Marshall. Living the university lifestyle comes hand in hand with a wild social life. However, once we finish our education, is when we grow-up and be more responsible." I pause before adding. "Well, most people do." I cast him a knowing glance.

"What are you implying?" he snaps back at me. I don't need to say anything. I raise a knowing eyebrow and a lopsided grin. He reads my expression perfectly, and it incites the exact reaction I was expecting. Not even a therapy session is required for me to know that Vance Marshall is a bear and doesn't need much poking to get a rise out of him.

"Imply would suggest that I was referring to a possibility." I refrain from showing any real emotion in my voice or facial expression. "When it comes to you, the tabloids have all the evidence that points to the truth. Some simply never grow up."

His face goes all shades of red, a clear sign that I'd hit that delicate wound that has already been rubbed sore by Coach Scully. I've just gone in with the salt. For a moment, I think that he's going to blow a gasket, and Lucy is watching us both. Her eyes flick between us like a tennis match, her expression makes me think that she wants to pole vault over Mars to escape from the confrontation. But then he surprises me when his demeanour suddenly changes, and his comeback is far from aggressive yet stinkingly patronising.

"Shouldn't you be at home sharpening your psychology skills for your first victim?" The cocky smirk on his lips tells me he's fully aware that he will be the first one to grace my couch. He's so infuriating. So much so that at this moment, I'd love nothing more than to reach over the table and slap that arrogant look off his face. But I know better than that.

"Not really," I offer back. "It's not like I can go into any detail of my past or present work due to client confidentiality, but I can assure you, I've dealt with all different levels of issues and behaviour and to be quite honest, my work here will be like a walk in the park."

Due to the lack of a response and any readable expression on his face, I get the impression that I've flummoxed him enough to force him to shut the fuck up. Suddenly he lets out a raucous laugh which makes Lucy almost jump out of her skin.

With his head and comment clearly in the direction of my newfound friend, no longer acknowledging me, he pulls Lucy tighter into the crook of his arm. "It was great to see you, Lucy. Maybe we should do this again sometime, just you and me." He finishes with a kiss against the hair at the side of her head before sliding off the seat and stands at the head of the table. "Better get back to the guys." When he turns to leave, taking a step brings him slightly nearer to me. Instead of continuing on his way, he stops and leans down towards me, his mouth coming close to my ear. My head tells me to jerk away from him, but my stupid body leans towards him. "Don't let the bartender get the better of you," he whispers. "But then you know what they say," I lean back so I can get a read on him. All I see in his eyes is contempt.

"Karma's a bitch and will come back and bite you in the ass." With that, he's gone, disappearing amongst the crowd.

I let his words bounce around in my head for a moment but quickly put them right to the back, take a breath and ask a simple question that I know will get the best answer.

"More drinks?" I ask Lucy.

"I'll get these," she says, jumping to her feet. "And when I get back, you can tell me what the fuck that was all about." I watch her while she wades her way towards the bar, thinking how the hell do I explain it when I don't understand what's going on myself.

CHAPTER 18

Saturday comes around before I know it, thanks to Lucy. After being reckless and getting far too drunk at the sports bar on Wednesday night, I'd crashed on Lucy's sofa. The next morning both of us had been nursing the hangovers from hell, so it was a good thing that Thursday was Lucy's day off from work. Once we downed a hangover recipe handed down from generation to generation in Lucy's family, which held raw eggs and pickle juice, she declared that the next best thing would be to get outside.

Lake McDonald at the national park was completely stunning, and although dubious at first as to how the hell it would help my pounding head, the crisp fresh air and beautiful surroundings did the trick. On the way back, Lucy pointed out a few places of interest. The mall, which is the biggest shopping complex I've ever seen, despite her assuring me that it was tiny compared to the ones in other states like Minnesota and California. A coffee shop, best supermarket and the library were also pointed out, not that I'll get much time to read anything other than case notes while I'm here, but it's still good to know. A couple of miles out from my apartment, we stopped at what Lucy reckoned was the best steak joint in Montana. Once I'd tasted the delicious, succulent beef, noisily cooing and moaning out my appreciation, I had to agree with her.

At the time, I hadn't thought Mars' dig in the sports bar had resonated with me, but it must have because yesterday, I found myself going over previous notes of a client from a year back who played football for one of the English clubs. It had been a complex case, a hard nut to crack. His love for the hard stuff, mainly whisky, had been problem enough, but when he'd started to dabble in drugs, it was obvious that things had escalated and become more serious. The club he was with at the time was pushing an anti-drug campaign, so of course, the chance of his antics becoming public was more than the club was willing to risk. Hence why they brought me in. The board had enough level-headedness to know that usually there's a reason why people act the way they do, and sometimes it's deep routed too. Over time or a trigger can suddenly cause their behaviour to escalate to epic proportions. Not only that, on a professional level, his antics were affecting his game, which in turn was on route to ruining not only his career but also his life. It had taken me six weeks to get him to open up to me.

Six weeks of us sitting in a room, face to face and him staring me out, trying to intimidate me into giving up. I didn't bow to his scare tactics. Shit, it was nothing on the bullying I'd endured in my school years. Once he started talking, all his childhood terrors came gushing out. It was clear that it was those experiences that had led him down the path that would lead to destruction. But after lots of hours talking, rehabilitation and putting practices into place, he had come out the other side. He was now one of my close friends, almost family, along with his wife and two small children. The trip back down memory lane prompted me to pour myself a glass of Gin and tonic and have a 'proud of myself' moment. I'd only taken a couple of sips when an idea had popped into my head. It was two-thirty in the afternoon, and when I'd pulled up the team's schedule on my phone, that Coach had kindly sent me on day one, I'd seen that on Fridays, at that time of the day, the team would be out on the training field running plays. Perfect.

Gin forgotten, I'd quickly swapped my leggings for a pair of ripped jeans and pulled on an oversize hoodie. I'd grabbed a baseball cap on my way out, made my way to my car and driven over to the training field behind the main stadium ground. With the cap pulled down low, my hair tied back, and inconspicuous dress, I'd found a spot where I could watch without being seen.

Memories of my days at Capa Down Academy school, hiding in the shadows as I watched Mars, Bell and the rest of the Capa Cobra's take the field for practice, had come flooding back. I was hiding then, and here I was seven years later, doing the very same thing. Watching Vance Marshall do his stuff.

I had 'wowed' to myself when I'd seen how fluid and precise Mars moved around the field. He oozes confidence and skill with every step, rush, and tackle. It's clear why he's one of the best Linebackers in his field. But what makes him so special, is that he's got the skills and ability that clearly show that he could take any position on that field and make it his own, and possibly outshine some of the best. He'd been good back when he'd played for the Capa's at only eighteen. Now at twenty-five, he is exceptional. I'd watched a few more plays being run before the practice had started to wind down. Back slapping, isotonic sports drinks and bottled water were handed around while Coach had gone over the points where he was looking for improvement. From what I could hear from where I'd stood, none of it was directed to Mars.

Suddenly, while I had been trying to catch the last bit of Coach's team talk, Mars' head quickly spun around in my direction. I swear he'd looked right at me, his facial expression giving nothing away, but hell, it was a little bit creepy. I remember when Mars had opened up to me and confessed that he'd known all along that I'd been there in the background, watching the Capa's training sessions. He'd told me that he could sense me, despite not being able to physically see me. I had watched them back then, but that was a long time ago. Could he really feel my presence now? Like I can feel him too?

Maybe it is some kind of weird juju or something? Empathy, Vibrational energy? Who knows, but I'm sure there's a group of scientists somewhere trying to get to the bottom of it.

When he'd looked my way, I'd quickly stepped back, not that it made much of a difference, because I was pretty sure he'd been well aware that I was stalking in the shadows. As soon as I was sure that his attention had gone back to the rest of the team, I'd made a quick getaway. Once safely back in my car and away from the grounds, it had occurred to me that, one thing was for sure, watching Mars play had still given me that same buzz. Whether it was while back in school or since then on the big screen, it gave me the weirdest kind of high that no drug or splash of alcohol could replicate. At that same moment, I'd also made a vow to myself. No more hiding.

Today I get to put that into practice. I have a legitimate reason to be on that field, standing beside Coach, and observing every single one of the team members. Because I've officially started my position as sports psychologist. No more holding back or hiding in the shadows, it's time to let them see exactly who I am, and especially Vance Marshall, how far from hopeless, Hope Palmer is now.

CHAPTER 19

When Monday comes around, I've already made my presence known to the team. Everyone seems to be accepting, and not one of them has voiced any negative comments. Not even Mars. Although I'm not sure that's the case when I'm out of earshot. The locker room is interesting, to say the least. A few of the guys have tried to intimidate me by stripping off or dropping their towels after being in the shower, purely by accident, of course. But if they thought that it would send me scampering from the room with embarrassment, then I've been there, had it done numerous times, couldn't give a flying shit. Nice view though.

When I'd handed out the schedules to the group that would include the three key elements of my psychology sessions, Motivation, Visualisation, and relaxation, some of the guys had got vocal, voicing that none of the subjects were relevant to them. They quickly shut up when I explained that not only were they expected to participate in the classes, but also Coach Scully and the fourteen assistant coaches that were an integral part of the fitness and mental balance were too.

It's blatantly obvious to me that as they all started to filter into the inside sports hall this morning, that the way that they're dressed, only a small proportion of them have read the subsections on each of the categories. Thick fabric tracksuits, heavy trainers and a couple are wearing club scarves and gloves. The last couple of days have been unseasonably cold for Montana, but Jesus, the heating systems that have been set up, which also pumps fresh, filtered air has the room temperature at forty degrees. Perfect for Hot Yoga.

"Damn," Dallas Rucker, the QB1, curses out at the top of his voice. "It's fucking hotter than Hades' nut sack in here. What the hell?" Unzipping the front of his track top, he shrugs it off and flings it dramatically across the room. No surprise there. I've already pegged Dallas as the drama queen of the team. Every team has one and, in the NFL, it's more times than not, the Quarterback.

"Aw diddums," T.J Burress, Running Back sniggers. "You worried that you might actually build up a sweat and your fake tan will start to run?" T.J is really hot, and from what I've seen so far, a little on the flirtatious side. I've caught him watching me a couple of times and as soon as he notices that he does nothing to hide it. His eyes shine and he flashes me the sweetest of smiles, showing his pearly whites. I won't deny that the attention he bestows on me has me smiling right back.

"What you spouting?" Dallas hollers back with a noisy hiss from between his blindingly white teeth. "This is all real, darling," he snakes his hand in front of his body from head to foot, and hell if he doesn't cock a hip too. In private, Dallas is very open about his sexuality, and all the guys are cool with that. In the public eye, Dallas keeps it under wraps simply to make life less complicated. Unfortunately, there's still a large part of the population worldwide that are judgmental. Being gay and into sports is not new, but when it comes to contact sports, unfortunately some are cruel with ignorance.

"Gentlemen," I say loudly, clapping my hands to get the group's attention. "Might be a good idea to read your schedules before the next session, so you can dress a little more appropriately."

"Yeah, douchebags," Buzzy, real name Guy Barker–Wide Receiver pipes up.

"Thank you, Buzzy." I press my lips together to stop myself from laughing because although his attire is more suitable, the lycra shorts he's wearing does nothing to mask the fact that his balls are way bigger than his cock. I internally pull myself together so as not to show my amusement.

"Welcome to Hot Yoga," I announce and in return I get a barrage of 'Huh's.' "It's been medically proven that if done correctly and safely, Hot Yoga can provide a number of benefits. Which includes improved flexibility, bone density as well as supplying a cardiovascular boost and reduction in blood glucose levels. Not only that, it is also a powerful tool to help reduce stress and ease depression."

"Sounds like a load of bollocks to me." I don't need to seek him out amongst the bodies, because his deep voice is so distinctive to me. But I do anyway, swiveling my body in the direction of the negativity until my eyes fall on him. He's stood, legs wide apart, arms crossed with a cocky one-sided smirk on his face.

"Well, Marshall, it's irrelevant what you think…" I fire back at him, which incites him to push back his impressive shoulders further on his already rigid body. "And honestly, you don't have to take my word for it that you will all benefit from this. But as you're all required to be present and take part in the group and individual tasks that I've set out and have been agreed with Coach and the club board, you'll just have to go with it." I keep my voice on an even keel, not wanting to give away my irritation at Mars' attempts to rile me up. The last thing I want to do is to get his back up and therefore cause a disruption when all I want is to get on with the class and hopefully prove my point. Giving Mars little chance to hit me with a comeback, I quickly turn my back to the whole group and press play on my iPod, making sure the volume is on high. Music booms out and instantly fills the room from the speakers that I'd requested be set up in each corner. I let the mood music play on high just long enough to cut out any chance of Mars responding with his infuriating negativity, then turn it down until it's at a soft, relaxing level and call out for them to find a place on one of the mats and start the class.

Other than the scathing glares from Mars, which are pretty much constant throughout the whole thing, the rest of the guys seem to take it all in their stride. Coach Scully throws himself into it with great gusto, and I can't help but think that's more for my benefit, making sure the rest of the team follows his example, rather than his own.

Once we've done a sequence of cool down stretching, I announce the end of the session and that the guys should hit the showers. "It's important for you to wash away the toxins that you will have sweated out. If not, then your body will absorb them back into your skin."

"And you'll stink like a prairie dog's butt hole," someone pipes up. I think Chris Boiman–Fullback.

"Guess you'd know all about that, Boiman," T.J sniggers, then flashes me another of his perfect smiles. The rest of the team burst out laughing at Boiman's expense. While this interaction is going on, Coach Scully makes his way to where I'm standing at the front. He's moving slower than usual and seems to have a bit of a limp. I guess his muscle groups have had more of a workout than they have in a long time.

"Well, I can honestly say that I enjoyed that," Coach announces loud enough so that everyone in the room can clearly hear, at which someone sniggers back, 'yeah, looks like it'. "Let's show our appreciation to Hope with a round of applause." It starts with just him, but soon the rest follow, and I find it unexpected, and a bit embarrassing and I let out an awkward laugh. I glance over to where Mars stands, again his arms are firmly crossed, but when he catches my eye, he switches to a slow, inflated and very patronising clap. I laugh and shake my head at his childishness which soon knocks the condescending sneer, that was playing on his lips, clean off his face.

"Thank you everyone, but no need. This is my job, and although some of the time I will take you out of your comfort zone and even push you to your limits…" I fix my gaze firmly on Mars' dark and fierce eyes, so he knows what I say next is primarily directed at him, "I can promise that I won't give up or walk away until I've finished what I've been solicited to do." Mars' face takes on a reddish tone, his anger clearing rising to near boiling point. He spins around so quickly that he nearly loses his footing, and stomps towards the door that takes you out into the hallway to the locker rooms and showers. But hey, I can't help poking that bear just a little more.

"Marshall," I shout at the top of my voice. Coming to a

sudden stop at the sound of his name, Mars doesn't even show me the courtesy of turning to face me.

"What?" he growls, his voice thick with pure animosity.

"I hope you've not forgotten that you have an appointment with me in my office in forty-five minutes. I'll see you there." His arms are rigid at his side, and when I notice him clenching and unclenching his fists a couple of times, I wonder if the bear is about to go apeshit. When he starts moving again, not even responding to my reminder, he nearly pulls the door off its hinges as he leaves the room. I don't deny that I have a sense of relief. I just hope that the shower he's about to take, washes away his bad attitude and temper along with his arseholery. One can but hope.

CHAPTER 20

I give Mars an hour, but when he still hasn't turned up at my office, I start to get pissed. One thing that I absolutely detest is tardiness. If you have an appointment, you make it. On time. Early, preferably. Not turning up that's a big no, no. Absolutely bloody disgraceful. In Mars' case though, not totally unexpected.

After checking with the front desk that Mars hasn't left the building, I check the common areas, like the dining room and chill-out zone. Even the gym comes up blank, so I make my way to the locker room. Mars isn't a prima donna and, unlike some of the team members, isn't one to spend a lifetime in front of the mirror making sure his hair is perfectly in place. So, when I enter the locker room and see that his sports bag and casual clothes are still in his spot, it comes as a surprise.

The only other door, other than the one I've just come through, is the one that leads into the bathroom area. When I get nearer the door, a subtle sound of splashing is enough to confirm that someone is still in there and as all the other pegs are clear, it can only be him. I push open the door and step into the open, white tiled area.

"If you thought this was a safe place to hide, thinking that I wouldn't dare come in here, you're greatly mistaken," I announce as I walk further into the room.

Mars is sitting in one of the large baths, and as I take a step closer, I can see that it's three-quarters full of ice and water.

"I'm not hiding," He responds, a slight judder in his voice. "I'm getting rid of the lactic acid in my body. Or did you skip the basics of your top-notch education?"

"I hope you showered before you got in there?" I reply, ignoring his dig.

"Of course I did. I might not spout about my knowledge or the dos and don'ts like some do," he stares pointedly at me, "but I've not got my body to this standard of excellence without knowing how to take care of myself."

"Pity you didn't take in the damage that alcohol has when taken in extremes," I counter. "You missed your appointment. Why?"

"Isn't it obvious? I need to take an ice bath."

"Really?" I challenge. My upper lip curls, eyes narrow as I look back at him with disdain. "I would have thought yoga would have been a piece of piss for someone with a body in such excellent condition."

"It was, but when I got out of the shower, I had this tight area here on my right calf," He leans forward in the bath and starts to rub his lower leg. "We have a game this weekend, so I thought I best try this first and see if it was enough to ease it up."

"Let me take a look," I say, stepping forward, my eyebrows knitted with concern that our star linebacker might be nursing a possible injury from my yoga class that could put him out of action. "It shouldn't be anything serious." When I get nearer to the bath, I see that Mars is wearing the tightest of shorts that leave nothing to the imagination. My eyes immediately fall to the crotch. Jesus, he's in ice cold water, and he's still got a distinguishable bulge. He lets out a snigger, no doubt catching me glaring at his goods, and as the heat hits my face, I snap my eyes away. "Show me where it hurts," I ask of him, leaning over the edge of the bath to see if there's any visible evidence of injury.

"Right here," His submersed hand goes as if to point out the area of pain. Instead, it comes out of the water, wraps around my upper arm, and before I've even had a chance to take a breath, I hit the ice-cold water with a splash. My head is fully submerged. I immediately drop my phone from my hand, and out of the corner of my eye, I see it hit the bottom. I place each hand on the floor of the bath and try with urgency to push myself back upright. But as soon as I get tenure, a hand lands on the middle of my back and pushes me further under until the rest of my body follows into the punishing cold. It takes me a few seconds of wiggling around before I get my head above water. The muffled laughter, while submerged, instantly becomes loud and raucous. My lungs feel like they're collapsing in on themselves as I struggle to catch my breath. My whole body is shaking, and not only because my skin is like ice. I'm in full panic attack mode, and despite having my head out of the water, I feel like I'm drowning.

"Oh fuck," I vaguely hear someone bark out, but I'm dizzy, disoriented and don't know what's going on or even really care. All I want is to be able to breathe. A feeling of weightlessness is followed by a softness that envelopes and warms me. "Come on, Hope, breathe with me. In, two, three. Now out, that's it. Follow me." Something clicks in my head, and I do as I'm told; somehow, my brain registers that it's the right thing to do. As my vision comes back, my wits become clearer, and I realise that I'm sat on the hard floor with my back to the bathtub. I focus on Mars, who's knelt on the floor in front of me, dripping water everywhere. I have one of the thick club towels wrapped around my body, along with Mars' muscular arms as he rubs his hands vigorously up and down my back, trying to warm me up. His deep chocolate eyes, which are full of concern, stare at me intently. "That's it, Hope." My hand is on his bare, muscular chest, and with every rise and fall I feel against my fingertips, I find myself breathing to the same rhythm. "You're okay; you're okay." I'm not sure if his mini chant is to placate himself or me.

"That was a shit thing to do," I mutter, through chattering teeth.

"Shit, Hope. It was meant to be a joke." The expression on his face tells me that he's riddled with guilt. "I'm sorry, really, I am. If I thought…"

"Mmm but you didn't think." I reprimand. The towel is lovely. The warmth generated from the friction caused by the constant rubbing of his hands is great, but his touch is doing things to me that I need to put a stop to. Our eyes hold on to each other. Our lips are too close. There is an unmistakable connection between us, still lingering and I know he feels it too.

"I need to get out of these wet clothes," I blurt out, shrugging out of his hold.

"I have a spare t-shirt and sweats. Let me go grab them for you." He vanishes back into the main locker room. My legs are still shaky as I make my way over to a stack of towels on the side and grab a couple more. With my back to the door just in case Mars comes back in, I ditch the used towel, along with my wet t-shirt and wrap the dry one around my torso, and the other around my shoulders, cape-like. Mars bursts back through the door with a club t-shirt, and sweatpants over his forearm and another item of fabric that I can't quite make out in his hand. He walks straight over to me.

"They'll be too big on you, but at least they'll be dry. I err… I've got you some boxers. I assure you they're clean." He unfolds the garment in his hand and holds them up to show me. They look remarkably small, which has me wondering how the hell they fit over his peachy arse, but then he pulls at the fabric, and they look to be super stretchy.

"Thank you," I reply. My hand is still shaking when I take the garments from him and when our skin touches, my whole body lets out a violent judder.

"You're still cold," he mutters, although I'm not convinced that it's the reason for my involuntary reaction. Well, he is still standing there, wet, topless. His soaked shorts stick to his body like a second skin and give me a perfect outline of his slack, but still very impressive, penis. I grab another clean towel from the stack and throw it over to him. I need him to cover up, as the task of keeping my eyes above his waistline is not easy. He catches it easily, and all hale to sweet baby Jesus, he immediately holds the corner against his chest as he dries his upper body, the rest hanging down and covering his man meat. "I'll give you some privacy," he says sheepishly as he hands me my very wet phone. "Sorry." He adds before he turns to make his way out of the room. "Once I've got dressed, I'll go grab you a hot drink from the vending machine, it will help warm you up." I'm about to tell him not to bother, but the doors have already swung closed behind him.

Come to think of it, the idea of being able to hold my hands around something hot is appealing. My mind quickly falls on clinging fabric around an aesthetically pleasing penis and just what it would feel like to have my hand around it.

Damn-it.

Mind. Gutter. Out of.

I leave it a minute after the door has swung shut before I strip out of the rest of my wet clothes and start drying myself off properly before pulling on the loaned garments. The boxers are surprisingly comfortable. The t-shirt is way too big, so I grab the hem at one side, twist it and tie it in a knot above my right hip, leaving the rest of the material to drape down longer on the left. The sweatpants are way too long, but with a few roll overs at the waist and a few at the bottom of each leg, I think I'll manage to walk without tripping. I may however have to keep a hold on the waistband when I move about.

Once decent, I pop my head around the door to see that the changing room is empty. When I get to Mars' spot, the seat is littered with stuff, and it looks like he's literary dumped the whole contents of his sports bag, so I drop down into the seat next to his.

I look down at the blank screen of my phone, then hold the button down on the side to power it up. Nothing happens, nada. This is a brand-new phone issued by the club that contains all the contact numbers of the players and staff. I press hard on the button a few more times, frustrated that I've barely had it in my hands and I've already fucked it up. A hand grabs my wrist, making me jump. I look up to find Mars standing in front of me balancing two takeout coffee cups, one on top of the other in his other hand. I hadn't even heard him come into the room. Which is strange because usually, I feel his presence. Could be the water still whooshing around in my head.

"You shouldn't try turning it on," he says, releasing my hand. "Not yet anyway." He hands me one of the cups, then after glancing at the mess beside me, drops into the next empty seat beside me. "You need to let it dry out first."

"The bowl of rice trick?" I questioned.

"That's doesn't always work, and you risk getting dust inside it. Your best bet is silica."

"Oh, right. Best nip down to the silica shop then." I say with a sarcastic smirk on my face. "How am I meant to do my job now?" I violently shake my hand that's still clutching the phone, as if it might miraculously make a difference.

"Here," Mars holds out his hand. "I know someone who can fix it. He's done it for me before and he usually gets it back to me the next day. I'll give him a call and drop it over to him."

"This has happened to you before?" I ask, dropping the phone into the palm of his hand. "Don't tell me, you dropped it down the toilet when drunk?" I snicker as I watch him get to his feet and move around to grab his almost empty bag from the floor. He slips the phone into a side pocket and zips it closed. His hand comes up and rubs the side of his forehead before he mumbles a response.

"Something like that," he replies. I try to catch his eye but he's avoiding all eye contact. It's a classic sign of embarrassment. The touching of the head, the inability to make eye contact, the definitive creasing of the brow. Well,

well, well. Vance Marshall's mask has slipped a little and has given me a glimpse of his feelings. I should really leave it alone, but the psychiatrist in me wants more.

"Sounds intriguing. Care to share?" Now he makes eye contact, and it's not very pleasant. The caring, concerned glimpse of the Mars that had shown its face, was now gone. Dark, narrow eyes shot at me like sharp spears trying to pierce my skin.

"I do not." He hisses back and begins vigorously stuffing the discarded items on his seat back into his bag. He doesn't even attempt to fold any of the items of clothing that's amongst the pile, and when I go to take one to do just that, it's ripped out of my hands before I even get a chance to shake it out of its crumpled state. I can tell his temper is on the rise. By the time he's onto the last few things, he's using his full fist to punch them into the over-filled bag.

"If you folded them, they might go in easier," I pipe up then clench my jaw as I try to hold the laugh that's bubbling in my throat. When his head swings in my direction, the muscle ticks at the side of his jaw, his knuckles white as he grips onto the side of his bag, the tension on the leather so tight that I'm sure it's about to pop every stitch, I can't help it. A laugh, snort, and blubber bursts out of my mouth and nose, and however much I try to hide it with my hand, he sees it.

"Fuck off," he growls at me as he slings the strap of his bag over his shoulder and turns away from me.

"As we still need to have that one-on-one session, and I know that your schedule is free for the rest of the day, I'll see you in my office in say, an hour." He stops, his hand inches away from grabbing the door handle to leave and turns to face me.

"You've got to be fucking kidding me?" he growls. I take the few steps needed with one hand clinging to the waistband of my pants until I'm stood by his side.

"I kid you not," I reply, tipping my head so I can look him directly in the eye. My voice is strong and determined when I address him further. "If you think your stupid, adolescent games are going to get you out of this Marshall, you are very much mistaken." I keep eye contact while I reach forward, flick the handle, and open the door. "One hour." I reaffirm, before I slip past him and into the hallway, leaving him behind.

CHAPTER 21

Despite my authoritarian command at Mars, I'm still not convinced that he will show up. But ever hopeful, I make sure that everything is set for when he does. If he does.

I've been sat in my high-backed chair that's strategically angled with the matching two-seater couch and armchair, all the while watching the hands click around the wall clock for the last five minutes. I know it's accurate within a second or two, which means it leaves Mars only three minutes until his sixty-minute deadline is up.

Not a minute more, nor a minute less, a pounding on the door makes me jump and rush with excitement in equal measure.

"Come in," I shout, even though the door is already opening. Cheeky fecker.

Mars steps into the room. His back is rigid, his chest puffed and instantly I know that his walls are up, and this is not going to be easy. Then again, I wasn't expecting it to be.

"Take a seat, Marshall," I gesture to the seating opposite me while keeping my eyes firmly on the open folder in my lap. He doesn't utter a word, but I hear the squeak of the soles of his trainers on the polished hardwood floor, as he moves into the room. When I raise my gaze just enough to can see his movements, as I would have predicted, he goes to the single chair, rather than the more comfortable couch, which would have been less restricting for his stature. Once seated, his broad shoulders fill the whole back of the chair, leaving very little space between his t-shirt clad biceps and the leather.

"I'm sure that you're aware of why these sessions have been arranged and what we hope to achieve from them." I tilt my head slightly; a subtle smile lingers on my lips as I do my best to defuse the building tension in the air.

"No idea," he replies apathetically. "Enlighten me."

I lean back into the chair, bringing my full attention to him, closing the file but leaving it still resting in my lap.

"Coach has already discussed this with you, I'm sure. But if you want me to explain again, then I'm more than happy to do so, if that's what you want?"

"Knock yourself out." He's doing his best to keep his emotions under wraps. Still, the way his arms are laid along the chair arms, his big hands cupping the end, and the rhythmic tapping of his index finger on his left hand against the leather, tell me that he's not as cool and collected as his voice and the rest of his body portrays.

I really want to bark at him that he's being a total childish dick and to get a grip, but I need to be professional about this and take out of the equation that this is Mars, and treat him like any other referral. However, I'm not going to pull any punches.

"The objective of these therapy sessions is to identify the reason behind your behaviour and work towards a resolution that will benefit you and your life going forward. The club is extremely concerned about your recent conduct and how it seems to be escalating. It reflects badly on both you and the club."

"And the club reckon you're the person to do that, huh?" he sniggers mockingly. "My conduct, as you so call it, is impeccable. I can count on one hand how many times I've given away yardage while I've been playing for the Longhorns and I've yet to pick up a fine, so this is all bollocks."

"The way you handle yourself on the field is not in question here, Marshall," I clarify firmly. "It's what you get up to in your private life."

"Exactly," he fires back. "Private life, which is my business and nobody else's."

I let out a deep sigh. "You know that's not true," I fail to hide the hint of sympathy in my voice, so I quickly continue. "When you are a hugely public figure, which you can't deny that you are, and have been for the past couple of years, every move you make on or off the field is there for everyone to see."

"You mean what they see in the papers, splashed across the news," he sniggers. "People don't believe that crap, because half of it is total bollocks anyway."

"Only half?" I shoot back with a raised brow. "Unfortunately, people do believe it."

"I don't see why I should have to change," he opposes, bringing his arms up across his chest in defiance. "It's not like I'm hurting anyone."

"But what the public see, including the younger generation that look up to you like you're some demi-god, is that it's fine to get legless, whore around and treat women with very little respect."

"I respect women," he mutters through clenched teeth.

"What, for one night only? You've never been seen with the same woman twice," I reprimand. "You might not have quick fumbles on the field, but you sure as hell have a lot away from it."

"What's up, Hope-less, are you jealous because you're not getting any? Didn't Bartender boy give you a seeing to?"

I really didn't want to rise to his downright obnoxiousness, but I sure as hell ain't going to sit here, however much I'm trying to stay professional, and take this disrespectful bullshit from him. Especially, while using the name that brings back memories of bullying and pain. Despite all this, I keep my voice level when I address him.

"First of all, jealous of your constant stream of one and done women? I don't think so. Two, you do not get to question my sex life, seeing as unlike yours, it's not splashed around by the paparazzi for all to see. Never going to happen, so not up for discussion and certainly no concern of yours."

Although the barman was cute and a bit charming, I had no intention of contacting him, but now. Maybe I should. Why? Who knows, but Mars mentioning it, plus the comment he made in the bar, makes me think that if I did, he wouldn't be too happy about it. Interesting!

I hold up my pointed index finger to stop Mars from speaking when he opens his mouth, ready to spout out a come back at me. I take a couple of breaths, then finish what I so eagerly need to get off my chest. "Lastly, quit the bully tactics, Marshall. Referring to me as Hope-less no longer has the effect that you look for. I'm no longer the easy target, I'm all grown up now, and if I'm not mistaken, you should be too. But as yet, despite your size and manly stature, all I've witnessed is pubescent, childishness."

"You can't fucking speak to me like that," he shouts, jumping to his feet. "This is a crock of shit, and I'm not putting up with it." He turns and storms towards the door which doesn't surprise me in the least. Jerking on the door, he pulls it open, but before he gets the chance to step through it, I shout out his name.

"I'll see you tomorrow at 2pm for our next session." I say firmly. "No more games, Marshall. I expect you to be here on time and minus the attitude."

"Dream on," he flings over his shoulder as he takes another step to leave.

"If you want to continue playing for the Longhorns, then I suggest you get on board with this, because otherwise," I sling back at him smugly, despite the niggling fear that sit heavy in my gut, " you're on borrowed time at this club."

My last comment must hit home, because he stands rigid on the spot for a few moments before he makes his move through the door, slamming it behind him.

CHAPTER 22

Mars surprises me when he turns up on time the next day, and to the Thursday session. But to be honest, it's a waste of both our time, because I get absolutely nothing from him. The whole hour is pretty much of us seated opposite each other and having a staring competition. When I do ask him a question, all I get back is a one-word answer. He certainly wouldn't win a game of 'Yes or No.'

Due to his reluctance, I end up cancelling the Friday session. If I wanted to, I could go and take my issue to Coach, air my annoyance at Marshall and how he's not open or willing to take the board's direction seriously, but I'm not one to give up that easily.

It's as plain as the gorgeous head on Mars' impressive, and hot as fuck body that there's something going on with him. I was hoping that one-on-one time, getting him to talk, would be enough to give me an insight as to what is inciting his reckless behaviour, but that isn't happening. So, my next step is back to basics. What most behavioural specialists would do when it came to a troubled child. Observation.

You see, even before I chose my vocation, I have always believed that external factors, traumatic events, the environment, peer input, etcetera is what influences us into being who we are. How we react to situations, emotions, and events in our life, because this is not a part of our make-up at birth. And ultimately, it's us that decides whether we follow the mould or break it. You know the saying; the apple never falls far from the tree? Well, in some cases, that apple decides that it doesn't want to be an apple; it wants to be different. A peach or grapefruit; something more than what they came from. Not that there's anything wrong with being an apple as long as it's not rotten at the core.

From what I know of Mars, the young Mars who grabbed my hand and opened the door that gave me the chance to leave behind my hideous, unbearable life is not rotten to the core. Somewhere along the way, his skin has been bruised and tainted, and I'll be damned if I won't at least give it my all to try soothe away the damage. The path he's on right now will only lead him to destruction.

Because I'm new to all this and have yet to find out about the player's haunts and general free-time activities, I decide to call on Lucy to help me with my next plan of action.

Of course, with client confidentially and all that, I have to be a bit cloak and dagger with my reasons for wanting to hit the same haunts as the players. But as Lucy and I have spent most days having coffee, drinks or just chilling at my place with a takeout, wine and Netflix, when I ask her if she's up for coming along on the away game this Saturday, she's immediately up for it.

The away game is against Denver, which is an 8-hour road trip. Yes, flying would be a tad quicker, but as the team can visit a brand-new state-of-the-art, training ground in Casper, Wyoming, on the way back that they are looking at using as an offsite training boot camp, using the club bus is the better option.

The plan is to travel down on Friday night, stay at one of the hotels near the Denver Mile High Stadium, so the team are fresh for the Saturday midafternoon game against the Broncos. After the game, another night in Denver with an early start Sunday morning up to Casper. A couple of hours looking around the new sports facility and then home. Our estimated time back in Billings is around 5 pm, giving the guys time to decompress before training again on Monday morning.

Saturday night, after the game is when I'm hoping that Lucy and I can get to shadow the players, specifically Mars. This is the only time they get to enjoy some downtime while we're away, so it gives us the perfect opportunity.

Lucy is'nt usually part of the entourage that gets to go on away games. Still, after I asked Coach Scully if she could join me on this particular trip as my assistant, without grilling me as to the reason behind it, I managed to bag her a seat near the front of the bus next to me. I'm not sure if Coach is happy to just give me whatever I want or if, in this instance, he was too focused on the game to give a flying fuck. I guess time will tell.

The general banter on the bus is playful and light, considering the amount of testosterone on it. Marshall is sat right at the back, and other than a couple of interactions with Buzzy and Boiman, he's quiet as a mouse. However, I don't miss the scathing glares he casts my way whenever he gets the chance. Halfway through the journey, despite wanting to avoid using the toilet, especially after the guys, I really need to pee. The toilet is about two thirds down the coach, and surprisingly I find it in reasonable order. After I've relieved myself and washed my hands, I step back into the centre of the bus and start to weave my way back to my seat. When the driver takes a sharp right, I lose my balance and fall sideways into TJ's space.

"Whoa," he grunts when my hand hits the top of his thigh, thankfully not on his junk, as I try to stop my fall. "You okay there?" he asks. His arm hooking around my waist and bringing me further over him and into his lap.

"Sorry," I gush out in surprise. I grab hold of the headrest in front of me, but when I try to use it as purchase to get back up, TJ' tightens his grip.

"No need to rush off," he says as he pulls me even tighter against him. I can feel something stir under my arse cheeks that's a little concerning but also quite intriguing. His mouth is close to the side of my head, his nose nuzzling in my hair, and I swear to God, he sniffs me.

"Mmm, you smell nice," he murmurs as he fingers my hair with his free hand.

This is not good conduct. I cannot be fraternizing with any of the players, coaches or management. It doesn't only go against my better judgement, but also my moral code. Do not mix business with pleasure.

"TJ, I need to get back to my seat," I say strongly as I try once again to pull myself up. I get about halfway, but TJ's not giving up so easy, and he pulls me back down.

"Burress," Mars' deep, powerful voice comes from just behind me. "Let her go."

"Ahh, shit, Marshall." TJ grunts before releasing his hold on me. "You're such a fucking spoil sport."

Mars gently takes hold of my upper arm and helps me get back on my feet and stood upright in the walkway between the seats.

"You, okay?" he asks me with a modicum of concern in his voice. His brows are down, two faint creases between them mark his normally smooth forehead.

"I'm fine, thank you," I smile back, marginally shocked at his act of concern.

"Then stop flirting with the team and fuck off back to your seat," he hisses at me before turning and making his way to the back of the bus.

Nasty fuck face.

CHAPTER 23

The sun is starting to set by the time we arrive at the Four Seasons hotel, which is about two kilometres from Sports Authority Field at Mile High. Already, the city is starting to sparkle with lights, and the hotel is one impressive addition to the skyline. Hopefully, with its fitness centre, spa and pool facilities, it will be enough to keep the team entertained in a healthy way before the big game tomorrow.

Bodies and luggage fill the foyer, and the noise as the players talk shit between themselves, some of them goofing around, is ear busting. But once everyone has been allocated their accommodation, the area soon becomes less crowded as they make their way to the rooms.

In situations like this, the guys double up in rooms with two double beds, so it seems only fitting that Lucy and I share too. Neither of us is particularly self-conscious about sharing the space, even though our friendship is fairly new. We've already seen each other in a minimal state of dress when I've crashed at her apartment.

The room we have is clean, spacious, and more luxurious than we need for our short stay, and the mountain view from the window is utterly breathtaking. We choose our beds, unpack what we need to for now and quickly freshen up, so we're decent enough to go down to the hotel bar for a drink.

We hit the bar just off from the lobby, and slip onto the white high stools in front of it and order a cocktail each. Lucy, a lover of bubbles, orders a Hugo Spritz - Prosecco, St. Germain, Soda water and mint. I order an Artful Dodger, which surprisingly in this joint is Hendricks, Orgeat, Absinthe, Dolin Blanc Vermouth and mmmm Lemon. Not the whisky or bourbon-based version that I've had before.

When the bartender slides our drinks in front of us, they look very sophisticated. Not an umbrella or glace cherry on a stick in sight. This is a classy joint and that makes me wonder why the hell they booked it for a bunch of jocks. Guess that's the difference when you're an NFL team.

"This is the first time I've come on one of the away games," Lucy giggles excitedly. "Thank you for making this happen."

"Don't thank me yet," I smile mischievously back at her while running my fingertip around the rim of the glass. "You have no idea what kind of shenanigans I might be getting you involved in. You might regret agreeing to coming at all."

"Oh, my goodness, what exactly do you have planned?"

"Well as you know, I can't tell you, because if I did, I'd have to kill you." I deadpan.

She nearly sprays out the mouthful of cocktail that she's just sucked up her straw, but manages to swallow it all before almost choking on a bit of the alcohol that must have slipped into her windpipe.

"Don't worry," I laugh at her stricken face. "I'm simply planning on watching the players on their down time. See how they interact with each other. Who gets on with who you know, see if there's conflict between any of them?"

"Ahh, you want to get a feel for them?"

"In some ways yes, but not physically. That would be more than my jobs worth. Observing them can tell me a heap of stuff. Body language, most of the time, is clearer to me than the spoken word." She nods her head as if she understands, but the way her brow is down tells me that she has no idea what I'm talking about.

"Yeah, but how? For example. How do you know if someone is lying?"

"Now that is an easy one," I shrug, but realise that I sound condescending. "For me it is, anyway. I've even done a thesis on it. Avoiding eye contact or doing strange things with their eyes is one sign. Being vague or on the flip side giving too much information. Unable to provide specifics or their story constantly changes. Mumbled responses when challenged. Then you get the little telltale signs such as playing with their hair, lips or put up a barrier by using hands, elbows between you and them, the crossing of the arms in front of their body."

"Oh my God," Lucy's eyes go wide. "You're so right. I wish I'd known this when my Ex was telling me that he wasn't cheating. I wouldn't have stuck around only to find out a month later when I caught him and the bitch in our bed."

"Ouch!" I grimace in sympathy. "You were living together too?"

"Yeah, in the apartment I'm in now."

"Shit, that must be tough. I'm not sure that I could stay in the same place after something like that had happened."

"Believe me. It is hard." Lucy sighs. "Every time I step in my bedroom, I get a flash back of his hairy ass bouncing up and down while he's rutting into her. At least I managed to trash the bed and get a new one. I'm trying to find somewhere else to live but it's difficult to save for a rental deposit which are crazy high while still paying rent. I'm still a quite a few hundred short."

"If you reckon you can get enough cash together in a couple of months if you're not paying rent, then the answer simple."

"I ain't sofa surfing. Can't anyway, other than a couple of female friends that would offer me a night on their couch, the only other people I know are the players. The kind of favour they'd want in return, however hot they are, I ain't willing to pay."

"Come stay with me."

"Really? But…"

"If you're confident that you can get somewhere else in the time I'm going to be here, then sure. The place is plenty big enough and to be honest, I would love the company."

"I'm not sure the club would sanction that," Lucy sighs, the usual upturn of her mouth dropping down. I see the hint of disappointment in her eyes, but then I quickly get distracted when I catch sight of someone with a distinctive, imposing stature. One that I instantly recognise, flashes speedily through the foyer and towards the exit of the hotel.

"Leave it with me," I gush, jumping off the stool. Lucy has the cocktail glass to her mouth, as she's about to take a sip I prize it out of her hand and drop it back onto the bar. "Come on, we've got to go."

With my hand tightly around Lucy's upper arm, I rush us both out of the hotel and onto the sidewalk. The air is cool and the shock of it has us both shivering.

"What the hell, Hope? It's freezing."

"Marshall. He's left the hotel." I search up and down the street and catch sight of him. "Look there, wearing a black hoodie and black jeans." I tug on Lucy's arm so she's right beside me when I move off to follow him.

"Are you sure its him? Coach always puts a ban on players leaving the hotel before a game," Lucy stammers between chattering teeth.

"Oh, its him alright, and he's about to get up to some kind of trouble, no doubt," I hiss back. "But the question is, where the fuck is he going?"

"I guess we're going to find out," she sniggers. I let go of my hold on her, sensing that she's totally on board with the stalking malarkey. "Damn, with those long legs of his, we're going to struggle to keep up."

"Speak for yourself," she sniggers. "Nothing wrong with my legs. But yeah, let's hope that wherever he is going, it's not too far."

After around ten minutes of gentle jogging, Mars takes a right down a side street, and both Lucy and I simultaneously pick up speed to catch up to him. But when we get to the end of the street he disappeared down, he's nowhere in sight.

"Fuck it," I pant out, breathless from the sprint.

"Look, this street goes on for miles, so he must have gone into one of the first few buildings," Lucy offers.

"Yeah, but which one?" I shrug, feeling foolish for starting this madness in the first place.

"Don't be such a defeatist. Let's take a walk down and see if anything stands out." I nod in agreement, and we take our time checking out the different buildings, doorways and signs, which gives us both time to catch our breath. We pass a coffee shop, a number of eclectic retail units and an estate/realtor's office, all of which are in darkness and look closed for the day. But when we get around halfway, there's a large door that looks to be a less highbrow hotel than the one we're staying at, which by the stream of light coming from under the closed door, looks to be open.

"Bingo," I cheer, clapping my hands together. "This must be it. Not sure why he's left a perfectly good five-star hotel for this… what? Three at best?"

"Err, Hope…" Lucy interrupts, instantly catching my attention. "This isn't a hotel," she says pointing at an inconspicuous brass plaque on the wall that I'd not even noticed. "This is a… men's club."

"You mean a strip joint?"

"Well, it doesn't say that on the plaque. It's called the Hot Honey's Gentleman's club, but yes, I'm sure that any dancing that goes on behind those doors are of the erotic type," Lucy sniggers. "Do you really think that he's in there?"

"Defo. And if I'm wrong and he isn't, I'll strip off myself and do a spin around a pole for a few dollars."

"Wow, you're that sure?"

"So much so that I'll even let you take pictures and post them on insta."

"Damn, you crack me up," Lucy laughs out loud,

crossing her legs like she might pee. "Not that it will come to that because it's not like, we'll be able to check."

"Who said we can't?" I give her a closed mouth smile that I'm sure looks sneaky and not so different to the clown from the horror movie IT. Hooking my arm around her waist, I push against the door. "Just follow my lead," I whisper into her ear before we step inside.

Despite the club's exterior being inconspicuous, the inside couldn't be more different. Gaudy, pinky-red walls, with huge gold mirrors and architrave, is like 'Bam' in your face. A large ornate sideboard and matching armchairs against the wall are in the same tacky colours. At the other side of the foyer is a dark wood counter with a lamp, and a phallic-looking ornament on it. The floor is covered in a deep piled carpet, and yes, you've guessed it, in a baby poop, mustardy-gold tone. Ceiling to floor drapes in blood-red that are tied back give a dramatic effect to what I assume must lead you into the main floor of the club.

"Can I help you ladies?" A tall, slim, and not wanting to be too judgmental, sleazy looking man behind the counter asks us before we get more than a few feet in.

"What's the entrance fee?" I direct at him.

"I think you must be mistaken ma'am. This is a not a night club."

"You have female strippers here, right?" He nods back at me, but when he opens his mouth to say something, I cut him off. "Well, that's what my girlfriend and I have come to see. Isn't it, darling?" I squeeze Lucy even closer and nuzzle her hair for added effect. "I promised my honey a lap dance, and that's exactly what my girl is going to get."

"I'm afraid that's not possible. This is a gentleman's club, women aren't allowed."

"That's a bit gender phobic, isn't it?" I let out an exaggerated gasp of shock. "And a little narrow minded might I add. Don't you know this is the 21st century and that gender equality is something that is taken very seriously? It's not like we're not aware of exactly what's going on through there." I gesture in the direction of the drapes. "Just because we don't have a penis, doesn't mean that as confident lesbian women we shouldn't be allowed to enter your establishment and take pleasure in watching beautiful erotic dancers." He opens his mouth again, but I don't let him get a word in. "Maybe I should speak to the manager, or maybe I should call my lawyer." My body language is one hundred percent mega confident and dominant. I ain't giving up until I get what I want, and I must be giving off the right vibe because the guy looks like he's about to shit a brick at the thought of being sued. He might possibly even throw in a free lifetime membership at this rate.

"No, no need," he flusters, waving his hands around. "Look, it's the regular members you see. They won't like it in the slightest."

"They'll like it even less if I get my legal team involved and screw this place for every penny it's got only for it to end up being shut down." I warn.

"Okay, okay. I'll let you in but please try not to attract too much attention."

"Look, I promised my girl some sexy dancers, so are you going to make it happen or what?"

"We have curtained off areas at the back of the room. It's where the dancers do private lap dances for the customers. Why don't I set you up in one of those and then I can arrange for a few of the girls to come on through and you can take your pick?"

I don't answer straight away. I'm enjoying making him stew for a bit longer. I tilt my head to one side and look up at the ceiling, as if contemplating his offer. God of earth, even the fucking ceiling is gold. "That could work, I suppose," I eventually respond. "Throw in free entry and drink a piece and you could have yourself a deal."

CHAPTER 24

As the room has subdued lighting, except for spotlights that hit the T-shaped stage in the centre of the room where two busty topless girls wearing the tiniest of G-strings are doing their thing, we manage to slip past the rest of the punters undetected. Which is a miracle in itself, especially when I trip, nearly going arse over tit while being distracted by one of the naked girls that is suspended hands-free, about two feet from the floor. The only thing keeping her from hitting the deck is her butt cheeks clamped around the silver pole. Bloody hell, talk about buns of steel. More like titanium buttocks.

Creepster, as I've decided on nicknaming the reception dude, suddenly stops before he pulls back a red velvet curtain and ushers us inside. The cordoned-off area isn't huge and consists of a curved faux leather sofa that, at a push, you could squeeze three or four people on with a small round table to each side. Nothing else, but then what else would you need for a private lap dance other than somewhere to sit and an actual dancer, of course.

"All the girls are busy at the moment, so I'll get one of the waitresses to come and take your drinks order. A couple of the ladies will be free in around twenty to thirty minutes, so I'll send them into you." With that, he turns to leave, making sure that the curtain is fully closed behind him.

"What the hell are we supposed to do now?" Lucy asks wide-eyed, her hands fidgeting at her side. "I'm sure as hell not going to sit down on that thing," she points to the curved leather bench, "Eww, can you imagine what bodily fluids could be still impregnated into the fabric."

"I don't even want to think about it," I agree, scrunching up my nose and faking a retch. "Right, you stay here, I'm going to check out the other booths."

"This is crazy," Lucy whisper shouts as she grabs my elbow. "Let's just go. Chances are Marshall's not even here."

"No way. He's here alright." I don't tell Lucy that I can sense his presence. I'm sure that's why I looked up at the very moment he was sneaking out of the hotel. It's difficult to explain and sounds mad, but it's like I can feel his energy when he's close. My skin begins to tingle, and goosebumps pepper my skin. I felt it then, and I can feel it now. "Look, you stay here, I'll be quick and if the waitress comes, tell her I've gone to the bathroom."

"Fuck to the no," Lucy snaps loudly. I shush her, but she ignores me and adds. "There's no way we're splitting up. I'm coming with you."

"Okay," I agree almost at once because, to be honest, this place is freaking me out, and I do believe that there's safety in numbers. "Stay close behind me and keep your eyes peeled for Creepster. If he catches us, I'm not sure I can talk our way out of this a second time, so we might have to make a run for it."

"Me to you, stuck like glue." God, she's so adorably nerdy at times.

I open the curtain just enough to peek out and see how the land lies.

Fortunately, there is no sight of Creepster, but I do notice a couple of dark-suited, big buggers standing at each side of the room, no doubt on duty in case any of the punters get too handsy. They seem to be pretty occupied with the rowdy men sat at the tables around the stage area, so I step out from behind the curtain and usher Lucy to follow.

Like a couple of prowling cats, we move from booth to booth, peeking around the curtains. We don't linger; it's not like I am about to take up voyeurism or anything. It's a quick look to satisfy my spider senses that Mars is not in that particular booth. When I step up to the last but one, that we can see anyway, my body reacts in the same way as it did back in the hotel bar.

"He's in there," I mouth to Lucy. "I just know it."

"Right," she mouths back, but I can tell by the raising of her eyebrows and the way her tongue clicks on the roof of her mouth that she's sceptical. I poke my head around the curtain, and sure as pricks have dicks, Vance Marshall is sat dead centre in the middle of an identical couch to what was in our room, oblivious to what might have been left behind prior to his arse hitting it. He's legs are sprawled wide open; his arms stretched across the back of the leather seating. Not one, not two, but three girls are showing him attention. Two of them sit at each side of him, while the third kneels between his open legs. Each of them swaying and twerking their bodies seductively to the sound of Move, Shake, Drop by Flo Rida. His head is slowly rolling from side to side, his eyes seem to be unable to focus on anything. There's a stupid grin plastered all over his face, his speech is slurred and garbled. He's obviously pissed out of his tiny mind, even though I'm lost as to how he could have got so drunk in the short time he's been here. When we'd watched him take off down the street earlier, he hadn't been staggering or anything. Guess Mars is a bit of a lightweight when it comes to drinking.

All the girls are focused on what they're doing and are oblivious to both Lucy and me as we step all the way into the room.

Soon it becomes clear why, when I watch one of the girls' hands fall to the waistband of his jeans, flick the button and start to pull down the zip. Flash, flash. The girl on the floor leans close, and another flash of light goes off. The slutty little cow bags are taking photos of his cock, no doubt so they can sell them for the highest bid to some paparazzi dirtbag.

I can already see the headlines

'Disgrace in Denver.

Infamous Bad Boy Vance Marshall caught yet again with his pants down the night before a major league game.'

I can't let that happen.

"Hey, bitches," I yell loud enough so they can hear me over the music. Not to give them too much time to react, I swiftly move towards the girl on the floor and snatch the mobile phone from her hand that she's using to record the evidence and, ultimately their meal ticket. "Does your boss know that you're taking pictures?" I sneer at her. "Cos, I swear to fuck, I saw a 'No photography allowed on these premises' notice on the way in."

"Fuck," the girl sitting on Mars' left shrieks out in surprise and jumps to her feet. "We weren't doing anything."

"I call bullshit," I snide back at her. Opening the photo app, I see that they have taken a handful of pictures. All of them show Mars in compromising positions, and it's clear to me that they have been carefully staged, all showing him with his eyes open and a stupid sexy grin on his face. The press and news channels would have a field day with them. From what I'm led to believe, Mars is on borrowed time unless he turns it around pretty quickly. This is certainly damning enough to push the clubs' board of directors over the edge and terminate his contract with the Montana Longhorns. "This is a fucking dirty trick, ladies." I stop on each image and quickly remove it because, honestly, it sickens me to look at them. "Do you know it's against the law to take photographs of someone without their permission?" Once I'm sure all the clips have been removed, even double-checking for any video and cloud storage, I hold out the phone to hand it back. "I suggest you think twice in future when you get a half-cocked idea like this again, because you're damn lucky I'm not calling the cops and hauling your arses through court. Now, you two," I point at the two girls that had been pawing Mars, "piss off and make sure that you keep your boss and the bouncers away from here; otherwise I might damn well change my mind." With a quick nod of agreement, they scoot towards the curtain and slip out. The third one goes to follow but I grab her by the arm and pull her back. "Not you. You can stick around. We need you to show us the back way out of here, so we can get out of this place undetected.

I unlock my phone and pass it to Lucy. "Call a couple of the guys. Get them to come down here. We'll need help to get this big lump of stupid back to the hotel without being seen."

"Who?" she asks, bringing up my list of contacts.

"You know them better than I do," I reply. "Which of them are likely to keep their mouths shut?"

"All of them it they think that they might lose the best linebacker the teams ever had. I'll ring T.J. He's more likely to answer the phone straight away if he sees that it's you who's calling."

"Why would you say that?" My eyebrows shoot up into my hairline. I know that T.J. can be a bit flirty, but that's just him. Isn't it?

"Doh! It's obvious that he's got a major crush on you."

"Bhaaa! Not likely. But if you think he's our best shot, then go ahead. Get him to grab whoever he's bunking with to come as well. Tell him to get a cab and ask the driver to wait outside so we can get going pronto. Tell them that under no circumstances can they let Coach Scully, the rest of the coach team or players get wind of this." I look back at Mars and wonder why the hell I'm letting myself get tied up with all this mess. But I know why. Because all those years ago, he stepped up to help me. This is my chance to repay the favour. "Oh, one more thing. Tell them to bring some cash, lots of cash. I have a feeling that we might have to splash a good amount of it to keep this under wraps."

CHAPTER 25

Thankfully, T.J brought Mack Conner with him because, by the time they got to us, Mars was comatose. Mack, the defensive tackle, was big and strong and exactly the powerhouse we needed. As per Lucy's instruction, they had come dressed in similar inconspicuous clothes as Mars, hoodies and dark jeans. So, with their heads covered and faces obscured, they were barely recognisable as two top Longhorn, NFL players. Mars was like a dead weight, but with T.J. and Mack's help, we'd manage to get him up on his feet, using themselves as human crutches. As I'd surmised, there was a back door that the staff used which led out to the side of the building, reducing the risk of us bumping into anyone while we got Mars outside and into the cab. T.J. and Mack had to all but carry Mars to the taxi with his feet dragging across the pavement. But eventually, we'd manage to squeeze him into the back seat, with Lucy and I squashed at each side of him, trying to keep him sat up and less obvious that he was wasted. Luck would have it that it was a five-seater, so T.J. and Mack grabbed the two jump seats and sat with their back to the driver. It's a bloody good job we'd all managed to go back to the hotel together, because getting Mars out of the cab had been twice as difficult as getting him in. T.J. managed to sweet-talk the concierge along with a big tip, of course, to let us in through the delivery entrance at the back. The service elevator had been useful too, with the task of getting Mars back in his room without any of the coaches or other players getting wind of it.

T.J. and Mack have just this minute dropped Mars' body onto his bed. Even though he bounced a couple of inches on the springy mattress, he didn't open his eyes or utter a word. He was well and truly out of it.

T.J. had called forward while we'd still been in the taxi to fill Buzzy in, who was bunking with Mars, on what had gone on and to work on how we were going to get Mars back into his room. Apparently, Buzzy knew all about Marshall's vanishing act and had been happy to cover for him. Dickhead. Well, now it was time for him to redeem himself.

"Jesus, what the fuck is wrong with him?" Mack asks with a scowl on his face. He's leaning over Mars; Buzzy stands right beside him as they both check out the state of him.

"He's drunk, and a lightweight one at that," I huff out from the other side of the room. "He can't have been in the club more that, what?" I look to Lucy for confirmation. "Thirty, forty minutes?"

"At the most," Lucy validates before disappearing into the bathroom for a pee.

"When we got to him, he was already wasted," I stand with my fisted hands resting on my hips, legs slightly apart, annoyed at the state Mars has got himself in, in such a short space of time.

"Nah, that can't be right," T.J. walks over to where Mack is standing over Mars to check him out too. "I've seen Marshall drink a ton of beer, hard liquor, the lot and you can barely tell. Sure, when he's drinking some of his behaviour is inappropriate but he's aware of what he's doing, even though I'm pretty sure he knows that he shouldn't. This isn't alcohol, this is something else, and I'd bet my right nut sack that he wouldn't have taken any shit like that knowingly."

"Do you think he's been drugged?" I gasp, taking up position on the opposite side of the bed so I can check him out too.

"He might be lacking in morals, and be a total jackass with the women, but no way would he risk getting pulled over a bad drug test. The club do random testing all the time. You do that shit; you might as well wave your football career goodbye."

"Then it must have been those slag bags that he was with in the club." Lucy adds as she comes out of the bathroom carrying a hand towel and a glass of water. "They must have slipped him something so they could get some dirt on him." She places the items on the bedside table along with what looks like a couple of Advil.

"Dirt?" Buzzy questions, already looking guilty.

"They were taking photos of him," I share. "The type of pictures that will do him absolutely no favours if they hit tomorrows tabloids. They'd obviously recognised him as soon as he got there and thought, 'Whoopie, chance to make some easy dollar', cheeky pole shaggers." I give Buzzy a fierce look. "Why the hell did you let him go out?" I snap. Buzzy jumps back like I've slapped him hard across the face.

"Hey, lay off him, Hope," T.J. comes to his defence.

"You know what a stubborn, arrogant ass, Marshall is. Hell, he's done nothing but be a dick to you since you got here. When off duty, Marshall does what Marshall wants, period."

"Well, Marshall needs to get his head out of his arse," I warn. "Or it's going to be well and truly on the chopping board."

"You seem to be forgetting what's more important here," Mack urges. "We need to find out what exactly he's taken and find a way to get it out of his system, otherwise tomorrow's game is going to be a waking nightmare."

"Holy shit," I groan. "I've no idea how we can do that without involving Coach Scully."

"Let me ring my brother," Buzzy suggests. "He's an ER doctor at Lenox Hill Hospital in New York. He's got some experience in dealing with drug users, he might be able to help."

"Do it," I say quickly, and at once, Buzzy opens his phone up and hits buttons and puts it to his ear. "It's worth a try, at the very least he might be able to tell us how serious this is and if we need to get Mars to a hospital."

The phone can't have rung for long before Buzzy speaks at speed. We all watch him as he walks over to Mars and starts feeding back information to his brother. Tucking his phone between his ear and shoulder, Buzzy takes Mars' wrist and places two fingers at the pulse point while checking his wristwatch. He then reaches over and pulls back his eyelids one at a time. Mars grunts out and rolls over onto his side.

"Okay. Thanks for that. Yeah, I'll give mom a call after the game tomorrow. Love you, brother."

Finally, Buzzy finishes the call and walks over to where we're all standing waiting for the news, good or bad.

"As far as he can tell without actually examining him, it looks like he's been given sleeping pills. His pulse rate is a little slow and his pupils are slightly dilated, but that's not uncommon and he doesn't think it's anything to be too worried about. Because he responded to my checking him out, he doesn't think that he's been given much more than a standard dosage."

"So, he's going to be alright?" I ask, desperate for a positive answer.

"Well, that's the problem," Buzzy does nothing to ease the tension causing a tightness across my shoulders. "It depends very much on what kind they've given him. If it's, say an Ambien, it has a short life and it should be out of his system in three to four hours. But…"

"I hate it when someone finishes with a 'but'," Lucy moans.

"If they've given his something like Valium, then it could take much longer before he's totally clear headed. On the positive side, it doesn't sound like Marshall has had the time to intake much alcohol which could have made this a whole different game."

T.J. grabs the wrist where Buzzy is wearing his watch. "It's 11.20 now, so all we can do is hope that he sleeps it off and he's clear headed before the team meetup at 9am. Otherwise, Coach is going to lose his shit. If this was anyone else, they might have been able to talk their way out of it, but Marshall, that ain't going to happen. His card is already well and truly marked."

"You guys need to go get some sleep, so at least you're fresh for the game." I turn to Buzzy. "Any chance you wouldn't mind bunking in with these two, just for tonight?" I indicate to T.J. and Mack. "I'll stay here and keep an eye on him, make sure that he doesn't have any adverse effects to the meds."

"Do you want me to stay too?" Lucy asks. "When he does wake up, chances are it ain't going to be pleasant."

"No, you go get some rest too. Tomorrow is going to be interesting to say the least. Don't worry about me, I can handle Mars."

One by one, they make their way out of the room, each of them checking that no one is hanging around in the hallway before they slip out, leaving only T.J. behind.

"Are you sure you don't want me to hang around and keep you company?" he says softly and with genuine concern as we hover in the open doorway. "Promise it will be all above board, no funny business."

"I'll be fine," I reply quietly with a smile. He turns to walk away, but before I've had the chance to close the door, he whisper calls my name.

"Yeah?" I poke my head back around the door frame.

"Mars?" he smirks. "I don't know what history there is between you too, but I know one thing. He's one lucky guy."

"History, yes," I admit. "Future, not a cat in hells chance." My words are resolute, but it pains my heart when I voice them.

T.J. casts me a dubious look before he turns and walks away.

Closing the door, I put my back to it and let my gaze fall on sleeping Mars. Despite his size and manly stature, he looks cute and vulnerable as he lays fast asleep in the fetal position. Oblivious to the fuck up that he's made and how devastatingly close he is to what could be a catastrophe.

CHAPTER 26

"Hope… Hope…"

I bat away the hand that keeps shaking my shoulder. "Ten more minutes," I mumble around the pillow that my face is squished into.

"Wake the fuck up, Hope."

Mars!

I shoot upright when I realise who it is cursing me out. "What, oh," I blink a few times to get the lingering sleep from my eyes. Mars is stood at the side of the bed, looking glorious, wearing nothing but grey sweatpants. His hair is wet, telling me he's been up and awake long enough to shower. The way his back is rigid, arms crossed purposely across his naked chest, and the scowl on his face as he glowers down at me tells me that he's not a morning person. "Morning," I offer around a yawn.

"What the hell are you doing in my room?"

"Don't worry, numb nuts," I snigger, swinging my legs over the side of the bed. "I'm not into midnight romps with comatose dimwits. Besides that, can't you see that other than my jeans that I took off, simply so I'd be more comfortable while sleeping, I'm dressed." When I stand, his eyes roam down the lower part of my body. Although I feel the urge to pull my t-shirt down so it covers more of my black lace knickers, I don't want to give him the impression that I'm embarrassed in any way.

"Where the hell is Buzzy?" he barks when he finally stops ogling my legs.

"Mars, give me a minute, will you? I need to pee and then we can talk." Aware that my bum is probably half hanging out of the back of my pants, with straight arms behind me, I flatten the backs of my hands over my cheeks before walking over to the bathroom.

Once I've seen to business, given my face a quick swill, seeing as I'd had the sense to remove my makeup last night, I walk back into the bedroom to face Mars.

He's already straightened up the sheets of the bed he'd slept in, and was now sitting on the edge facing the one I'd just vacated.

"Can you remember anything about last night?" I ask as I walk over and sit opposite him.

"Some," he replies, rubbing the palm of his hand over the top of head. "But not everything." His eyes narrow as he's trying to recollect last night events.

"Why do you keep doing this to yourself, Mars?" I sigh, concern in my voice. "It's clear that playing football is what you live for, but you continue to risk it all with your reckless behaviour."

"Is that why you're here, to give me a lecture? Because if that's the case, you're wasting your time."

"I'm here trying to save your self-destructive arse, you... you..." I puff out an exasperated gasp. "Those three dancers you were with last night, slipped you some sleeping pills, got you so far out of your head then manipulated you into compromising positions and took photos. At one point they even whipped out your dick, so they could get the money shot that would keep them in hooker heels for the rest of their lives."

"Shit!" he puffs out loudly through gritted teeth.

"Yes, Mars. Shit," I snap back at him. "However, if Lucy and I hadn't decided to follow you, then fuck knows what might have happened."

"You followed me. What the hell, Hope?"

"What do you expect me to do?" I fling my arms up before letting them drop back to my side. "You won't talk to me; you blatantly refuse to engage in anything unless Coach Scully is around. I'm here to do a job Mars, and I take my work seriously. So, if stalking you is the only way I get some kind of insight as to why you are constantly trying to commit social suicide, that's what I'll do."

Not a word is spoken as a full-on staring match between us goes to hyper mode. Both of us are as stubborn as each other, so when he's the one who finally breaks the silence, I'm shocked.

"Do they still have the pictures?"

"I'm confident that I erased them all from the phone and backup," I reply. "We paid off the cabbie, and the hotel night staff that let us through the back way too, so they shouldn't say anything."

"What about the girls? Could they be a problem?"

"They no longer have any evidence, and I'd doubt that anyone would believe them without it." Here's hoping anyway after all the effort we've gone to. "But who knows? Only time will tell if we got away with it, but I'm hopeful that nothing is going to hit the media."

"I thought the way I was dressed would keep me

under the radar." Tiny beads of sweat pop up on his forehead as his breathing quickens. He's dropped a major bollock and he knows it. "I even insisted on a private booth so I wouldn't risk being recognised in the club."

"So, you do remember some of last night?" I question.

"Like I said, bits and pieces. When I got sat in the booth, I ordered a single malt, and was about halfway down it when the three strippers came in. I'd requested two, but hell, if it was buy two get one free, I wasn't going to turn it down." He rubs his forehead with the palm of his right hand. "The last thing I can remember clearly is the girls dancing around me. One of them handed me my drink, telling me to drink up so they could get me another. After that, everything becomes hazy. They were dancing, sticking their tits and arse in my face then… Damn, was Lucy there?"

"She was with me," Bastard. He can remember Lucy, but has no recollection of me?

"Jesus, everything's so mixed up. I can vaguely remember seeing your face, but then… that's crazy."

"What's crazy?" I lean forward, desperately wanting to know what he remembers about me.

"It was like your head, but not on your body."

"Are you trying to tell me that you saw me as one of those whore bags?" I seethe. "You're delusional."

"Hey, don't take it personally," he laughs as if it's just one big joke to him. "I was drugged, and everything must have been getting mashed up in my brain. Although with you being a short arse, you could probably do with a pair of hooker heels."

"You're a dickhead, Vance Marshall," I jeer back at him, grabbing my jeans from the bottom of the bed where I'd left them last night. "I should have left those photos exactly where they were and let them sell them to the highest bidder." I throw myself up onto my feet, so I can leave, but as I turn to walk towards the door, I don't get far as Mars' hand catches my wrist.

"There's just one other thing that I sure as hell can't get my head around," he states, holding me in place so I can't escape. "Why, when all I've been is a total arsehole to you since the moment you got here, when you could have easily hung me out to dry, you went out of your way to help me? Why, Hope, why would you do that?"

Up to this point, I'd given him my back, not wanting to face him due to the tears that had been building and were now threatening to overflow. But I can't keep it inside me any longer. The one unresolved issue that has been festering along with the memory we both share, needs to be exposed and excised once and for all.

"I'm here because I'll be fucked if I'm going to let you throw away all that you've achieved, all that you've worked so hard for. Everything that you dreamed of, what I wanted for you so hard, that I was willing to forfeit my chance with you when I walked out that door, seven years ago."

"Hope," he growls from deep in his throat, as he pulls me towards him. When he falls back onto the bed, he takes me with him, flipping us both, so I'm the one laid on my back. "You should never have walked away from me," he murmurs, looking deep into my eyes. "I was willing to give up everything for you, everything, so we could be together."

"Don't you think I know that?" I choke out, tears sliding from my eyes, down my temple and into my hair.

"But don't you get it? I couldn't let you do that because I was broken, I had nothing, and I wasn't about to drag you into my fucked-up life. I couldn't be the one responsible for fucking up yours too. I couldn't live with that."

"Jesus, Hope," he hisses as his hand palms the back of my head and brings his lips down to mine. In an instant, I'm right back in that hotel room when he kissed me for the first time and declared how much he cared. Back then, it was sweet and gentle. Now it's hot and hard. His mouth takes control, his tongue pushing through my parted lips and making all kinds of dirty advances on mine. "Fuck," his voice is throaty with arousal, which is also clear when his hand on my back moves down to my butt and pulls me tighter to him. He's so fucking hard. "I've wanted to do this since you turned up in the locker room that first day, but I was still so fucking mad at you for leaving me, that I couldn't let my defenses down." I want to ask him so many questions, I want to tell him so many things but when he kisses me again, I'm lost for words.

Mars hovers barely an inch above me, using his elbow and strong thighs as leverage. The hand that had been squeezing my bum cheek had now moved around to the front and is caressing the skin along my hip, stomach and thigh. When his fingers slip under the waistband of my knickers, I take in a quick, sharp breath and hold it, only to push it out when he cups my pussy. "Mars, I…" my hand wraps around his wrist, and I waver between telling him to stop, or demanding more. When a finger slides through my lips, hitting my clit, all thoughts of putting a halt to this are gone. "God, oh my god, yes." I find myself spewing out like a porn star when he slides a finger inside me. "Mars, we shouldn't…"

"Like hell we shouldn't," Mars, growls at my half-hearted attempt to put a halt to this, "I've waited seven years to get my hands on your sweet pussy, and I sure as fuck ain't stopping until I've had my fill."

"Bloody hell," I squeal when he adds a second finger to the mix and, without any difficulty at all, hits me right in the spot that makes my toes curl and my ears ring. "Oh, oh, yes… right there." He continues to stroke me until I'm so close that I can't stop my verbal outburst. "Oh my God. Holy fucking hell, Mars. I'm going to come, ahhhh…" The orgasm that hits me is what you find in a dirty romance novel, something that I never thought actually existed or ever experienced. And when I think that I might finally catch my breath, Mars moves down the bed, slides out his fingers and replaces it with his hot, wet mouth. "No, no Mars, I don't think–"

"Don't think, just enjoy," he says around my pulsing pussy, his tongue delving deep inside me as he begins to taste me. "You taste and smell fucking incredible."

When I'm about to be hit by a second orgasm, he pulls away, and I whimper out with frustration.

"Hold on baby, I just need to grab protection."

"Get a move on then, because I need you inside me," I demand.

"Dirty fucking girl," he sniggers huskily, but the crinkling sound of a packet being torn tells me that I'm not going to be left hanging for long.

When he pushes into me, I nearly die from utter bliss. The feel of him is so exquisite that I almost want to cry.

"Oh fuck, Hope," Mars groans out, his voice so deep and delicious that I want to fall into it and never come up for air. "I've dreamt of this moment so many times, but not once did I ever image how utterly perfect you'd feel wrapped around my cock." He moves slowly, bringing himself all the way out until only his tip is inside me, before thrusting back into me deep and hard. My God, he fills me perfectly, like we were meant to be. When he begins to pump harder and faster, all the while palming my breast and nipping at my nipples, causing a rush of blistering heat directly to my core, I feel my pussy start to contract as my arousal builds, moving quickly towards another breathtaking release.

"Hold on baby, don't come yet," he growls out as he grabs both my hips, fingers biting into my flesh in the most delicious way, giving him purchase to pound into me even deeper, hitting the spot that you can only describe as pleasurable pain. "Fuck, Hope. Fuck…" Letting go of one of my hips, he slides his hand between us, and between finger and thumb, he clamps a hold on my clit.

The mixture of his deep guttural groans and my high-pitched cries are like a sexy screaming rock chorus, and when it comes to an end, we collapse side by side, chests heaving, breaths frantic.

"Come here," Mars commands with his husky sex laced voice, his arms curling around my waist and teasing my body up close against his own. "You're one fucking mind-blowingly sexy woman, Hope Palmer, do you know that?"

"Better than what you've had before?" I joke but then want to kick myself for even bringing up the subject.

"I'll admit that I'm no saint, Hope. But please don't jump to conclusions from what you've seen in the tabloids. I've not slept with that many women. The media know how to manipulate a photograph, get the right angle, taking a reasonably innocent picture and making it look like it's something that it isn't." I tilt my head so I see his face because this is when I really need to read him. "I had a girlfriend or two back in college, not at the same time might I add. Most of the time I just fooled around because I didn't have time for a steady girlfriend. I was too busy making sure I kept my grades up so I could keep playing football. However, I'm not the man-whore that the media would lead you to believe either. The only thing I'm guilty of is not committing to one woman, but that was because the woman I wanted to commit to was long gone."

"Was it one of the girls you met in college?" I ask, wanting to know who made such an impression on him and held him back from getting close to anyone else. I also need to know who I might have to beat the shit out of if ever they turned up on game day.

"It's you, you dope. No women could ever make me forget you." The honesty in his eyes is blinding. "I was devastated when I woke up and found you gone, that's a pain I never wanted to feel again, so I did what I had to do, I protected my heart."

A rush of regret waves over me, so huge that I think I might drown.

"God, I'm so sorry, Mars. Truly, I never wanted to hurt you, never. Walking away was hard for me too. The thought of you not following your dream because of me was far worse." With my hands placed on his chest, I push myself up so I can look down on his beautiful face. "If you'd ask me if I regret doing what I did, I'd have to say no. Look where you are now, Mars, you are living your dream, or you will be if you get your arse out of bed because, if I'm not mistaken, you're late for breakfast with Coach Scully.

"Aww, shit, what time is it?" Mars curses, "Where's my fucking phone?"

Jumping out of bed, I walk over to where his pants are in a pile on the floor at the bottom of the bed, where he'd kicked them off before giving me the best seeing to that I've ever had. I shove my hand in the pocket that is obviously holding his phone, due to the weight at that side. "Here," I throw it to him, and he catches it one handed.

"Damn, it's 8.45 which gives me fifteen minutes to get showered, dressed and down there, although I could go down there with eau de la Hope Pussy on my skin. Might give T.J. the message to keep the fuck away."

"Mars, you wouldn't, you smelly bastard. Now go get a shower."

"You should shower too, otherwise Marshall cologne could give the game away."

"Shit, Mars," I grimace as the realisation of what we've just done hits me hard. The no mixing of business and pleasure has clean got out the window. This could jeopardise my work here. "We can't tell anyone about this. I've been brought in as your behaviour counsellor not your sexual one."

"Baby, even I have to admit that both of them are pretty much the same." When he laughs it's like music to my ears, but I'm also mad at how apathetic he is about it.

"Mars," I plead. "You can't say anything." I grab hold of his arm tugging on it until he looks me in the eye. "We need to keep this under wraps. I could lose my job over this."

"Okay, okay," he placates me. "I'll carry on being an arsehole to you, on one condition." Here comes the demands. "You agree to spend time with me whenever you're free"

"I think I can go with that," I smile at him sweetly. "But only if you agree to take your counselling sessions with me seriously and you start to talk."

"Damn, you bargain hard woman, now get your arse in that shower, so I can have another five minutes of eyeing up your sexy as fuck body without me getting that butt kicking from Coach for being late."

CHAPTER 27

Mars was late by thirty minutes, which he's adamant was partially my responsibility due to, as Mars put it, 'depriving him of seven years' worth of hard shagging my hot as fuck body of which he was determined to be recompensed for'. In other words, we had the most incredible shower sex, and took extra time in checking out each other's bodies. To be honest, it was a struggle to force him out of the cubicle before our dirty antics had us looking like a pair of over ripe avocados.

As soon as I stepped into the room I was sharing with Lucy, she came rushing out of the bathroom with a makeup brush in one hand and a compact of what looked to be fixer in the other.

"Oh my God. I've been texting you, but you didn't respond. I was worried that you'd stuck each other with a knife or something." Despite trying desperately to hide the fact that I'd just been well and truly fingered and fucked, she immediately picks up on the change in me. "Oh yeah," she singsongs when she sees the stupid grin on my face, and how I'm walking with my legs slightly apart because my pussy is still tender from all the delicious penis pounding it's taken. "Looks like I'm right with the sticking bit, but sure as hell not with a knife," she wiggles her eyebrows at me. "You two were introducing Dick to Clit, weren't you?"

"Jesus, Lucy."

Woah now. What on earth has happened to the shy, nervous young women that greeted me on my very first day here. Oh yeah, she's been hanging around with me. Bad influence.

I didn't want to lie to her, so I worded my response carefully. "Where the hell did you pluck that notion from?"

"It's obvious there's a connection between the two of you. The way you react with each other. The sly side-eye quick glances when the other isn't looking. Not to mention the ruse to get me to stalk him with you," she sniggers. "Research purposes, my ass."

"You're seeing things that aren't even there," I counter. "And the observation, that's true, and you know it."

"Hope," she sighs. "Stop trying to fool yourself. You might be the expert in picking up body language but I'm not totally clueless. I've read enough second chance, enemy to lovers romance books to recognise what's really going on underneath the banter and snide remarks charade. I don't know what's gone on in the past that got you both putting up barriers, but they sure as hell got smashed to smithereens last night."

"This morning, actually," I correct her with a smile on my face and a hint of a giggle in my voice. No point trying to hide it; she's clearly read the signs. Signs I hadn't seen myself. Bloody hell, maybe I need to go back and redo that part of the syllabus. "A few times actually."

"Woo-hoo! No wonder you're walking like a Texas rodeo rider." Lucy grabs my hand and pulls me over to one of the beds. With firm hands on my shoulders, she guides me to sit on the edge before bouncing down right beside me. "Seeing as being at the morning meeting is optional for us, and we don't have to be at the stadium until around 1pm, start talking, I want all the juicy details." Lucy stands, apparently deciding that sitting opposite me rather than beside me is the better option, flopping down on the adjacent bed.

Oh my God. Has this body language thing intrigued her so much that I've ended up created a monster?

"But first, I've got to know," A blinding smile takes over her face, and for once, her hands stay firmly by her side. With a wiggle of her eyebrows, the sparkle in her eye is of pure mischief when she asks, "Is his junk in proportion with the rest of his body? Because he's sure one big mother fucker?"

"It's going to be an epic battle on the gridiron today between these two NFL teams, Jeff."

"It certainly is, Cory. Whoever wins today will be guaranteed a place in the playoffs, and a chance to make it all the way to the Superbowl."

I hand Lucy her bucket-sized cup of diet coke, and tray of cheese-covered nachos, before falling into the seat beside her.

"We have a record crowd here at the Mile High

stadium, and the atmosphere couldn't be more electric," the voice of one of the commentators, I think it's Cory, sounded in my ear, but to be honest, they both sound very similar.

I only have one wireless ear pod in my ear that's connected to my phone, so I can listen to the banter of Jeff and Cory, while still being able to experience the mega hype of the crowd.

"It's about to start," Lucy gushes, her feet doing little giddy stomps on the floor beneath her. "This is so exciting."

"You go to the games all the time," I laugh at her over-enthusiastic eagerness.

"Home games, yes. But this is the first away game I've ever been to." She grabs onto my arm, giving it a shake, her face suddenly deadly serious. "I'm not asleep, am I? Please, tell me this isn't a dream." I reach out with my free hand and pinch at the skin at the back of the hand that's still gripping onto my arm. "Ouch!" she cries out.

"Not a dream," I laugh back at her. She rewards me with a dark scowl, which only makes me laugh all the more.

A voice booms out over the speakers as the usual rigmarole begins.

This bit normally has me fast-forwarding if recorded. You know, the teams coming out, the refs, it's all a waste of time in my eyes. I've often been known to shout at the TV screen to tell them to get the fuck on with it. However, when I see the unmistakable image of Mars as he jogs onto the field, my fucking heart flutters like it's caging a million and one songbirds that are desperate to fly free.

It should be all about the game and not all the boring stuff in between. I absolutely adore the game, but the breaks in between plays are too drawn out. That's one thing that's a major plus on English football, or soccer as they call it over here.

That's why listening to the commentator makes the breaks in between plays that bit more tolerable. Did I mention that these guys remind me of Ant and Dec? Annoying as shit, but you can't help but laugh at them.

The coin has been tossed; the Broncos captain calls it and chooses to kick-off to start the game.

The kick is made, the ball is in flight, and the Longhorns Running Back, the one and only T.J. Burress, waves his hand up high to signal a fair catch before receiving the ball, and the crowd go wild.

Game on.

The Longhorns certainly play as a team. They can pre-empt each other's moves like I've never seen in any walk of sport.

The whoosh of pride I get when the commentators talk about Mars, is so profound that it brings tears to my eyes and a lump in my throat. Whenever it happens, I make sure I take a big suck through the straw in my drink, so that if Lucy catches me being all pathetic, I can blame it on the fizziness of the drink for making my eyes water.

"Playing on the outside, Linebacker, Vance Marshall has flourished under the 3-4 defence. With his size, he's been great against the run, and with his speed he's been able to drop back into coverage and play well against the pass."

"With it being third down and only two yards to go, the Longhorns have put eight in the box to help stop the rush and prevent the Broncos first down."

By the time they go in for the third quarter, the Longhorns are up 36 to 10 and smashing it.

"Oh no it's a fumble by the Broncos, and look at that, its quickly picked up by the Longhorns defensive tackle, Mack Conner."

"Surely, he's not going to get more than a few yards before he's taken down?"

"Oh wait... This is crazy play, Jeff, he's handed off the ball to no other than Marshall, and holy smokes, look at him go. He's getting through the Broncos offensive line like it's just a walk in the park and damn it, he's not only gone and picked up a yard, but he's stopped a fourth down conversion."

"Cory, that guy is a phenomenal player. Marshall is one of the most effective Linebackers I've ever seen. Not only does he manage to surprise us all with plays like that, but he's able to penetrate the line to stop the run, but also has the speed to cover some of the best tight ends in the league. It's just incredible."

I can't hold it back anymore, and I no longer gave a shit if Lucy, or anyone else for that matter, sees me blubbing like a baby. The tears flow, and I'm a total mess.

CHAPTER 28

When we got back from the stadium, the hotel didn't know what had hit them when we all piled into the bar. The team, coaches, support team, and of course me and Lucy, as soon as we got back from the stadium. It was only right. There was celebrating to be done. A glorious 58 to 10 win has taken the Longhorns one step closer to the Superbowl.

When the game had finished, and I'd stopped being such a soppy bugger, both Lucy and I had cheered our little heads off, waving our arms like a couple of loons. While the team did their own celebratory back-slapping, victory dance and the like, Lucy grabbed my arm, pulling me out of the seating area and into the walkway that led you out of the stadium. However, we had no intention of leaving because, as we had passes that would give us access to players' areas, she insisted that we should wait outside the visitor's team changing room to congratulate our lads in person.

I must admit, I couldn't wait to see Mars, but I'd also been aware that it would hurt like a fucker when he'd rebuff me, even though it had already been agreed that's how it had to be. So, no one was more shocked than me, when Mars came marching purposely towards me, wrapped me in his arms and lifted me at least a foot off the floor. My mouth was still slack, and hanging open in shock when he spun us both around on the spot. When he'd eventually put me down, at least half the team looked at us in shocked horror as if we'd stripped naked, and were singing and dancing to Baby Shark. When eventually they'd turned away and started making their way into the locker room, I had hissed in his ear, "Way to go on not rousing any suspicion." To which his response was to take my mouth in a heated kiss, before informing me that he'd booked an extra room at the hotel, and that if I texted him later, he'd tell me the number.

All I can say is thank God Coach Scully and the rest of the support team were still dissecting the game with their Denver equivalents. Hopefully, Mars had convinced the team that his show of interest in me was just a way for him to fuck with the shrink's head.

Now everyone is here in the bar, so I'm grateful that, other than the casual glimpses in my direction from the other side of the room, that, by the way, heats me up all the way down to my toes, he's being very discreet.

Lucy is talking to Julia, one of the physios that always travels with the team, so I take the opportunity to pull up Mars' number on my phone, and punch out a message to him.

Me: Hi, it's me.

Marshall: … … … Who is this?

I stare at the screen, then look over to where he's standing with T.J. Buzzy, and Dallas. He's already watching me, so I quickly drop my gaze back down to my phone.

Me: You are suck a dick.

Marshall: If I remember rightly, it was you that sucked my dick. In the shower. On your knees, right after I had my tongue so far in your sweet cunt, I could nearly feel your tonsils.

I blink a couple of times at his dirty, sexy, no absolutely filthy but not untrue response, before I realise that auto text had switched out such for suck. "Oh, shit sticks," I mumble.

"You okay," Lucy asks me when she hears me cursing.

"Yeah, no. Yeah, I forgot to call my aunt yesterday when I said I would. No biggy, I'll message her, tell her that I'll give her a call tomorrow."

"I'll remind you." God she's so fucking adorable. I nod back at her and smile before going back to my phone. At least my little lie gives me an alibi for being on my phone. She'll think I'm just gabbing away to my aunt.

Me: I didn't hear you complaining.

Marshall: If I had, you wouldn't have heard me because you were enjoying having my cock in your mouth so much that your moans of arousal would have drowned them out.

Me: Is this your feeble attempt at sexting me????

With the unnecessary added question marks, I add a couple of emoji faces. The eye-roll one and the one with the round open mouth and wide eyes, which looked more like a blow job just before it goes to pop over the head of a cock.

Marshall: Room 402
Me: Wait.
Me: … … … What?

Me: That's a presidential suite

Marshall: Sure is, and I intend on making the most of it. There's a key card at reception waiting for you. You'll need it to be able to get to that floor in the lift. I'll see you in an hour.

"Hey, you okay here with Julia?" I interrupt Lucy.

"Sure why, you okay?" she asks, her face creasing with concern.

"Yes, I've got a bit of a headache and this rowdy lot ain't doing me any favours." I drop my focus to the front of my Longhorns jersey, and pick at the invisible piece of fluff that's not there. If I don't look Lucy in the eye, it won't feel like I'm deceiving her as much. "I have something I need to do upstairs," not a total lie, "before my next one-on-one session on Monday." Already having spent far too much time inspecting the front of my top, I lift my gaze to Lucy's face.

"Sure," she smirks. "Make sure you're all fired up, you know. Ready for them when they come at you hard." The knowing twinkle in her eye tells me there's no fooling her. She knows exactly what I'm up to, and who I'm going to be hooking up with. "Don't worry if you're out… of it when I come up later. I won't disturb you. I'll be as quiet as a mouse." She does an exaggerated wink, fortunately on the side that's away from Julia's view. I must admit, Julia doesn't seem to be perturbed by Lucy's strange, cryptic ramblings.

"Okay, well I guess I'll see you in the morning. When I wake up. In the next bed." *Oh, shut the fuck up, Hope,* I chastise myself, when Julia casts me a weird look. *'You're making it even worse.'*

"Don't forget to take a couple of Advil," Lucy quickly interjects, causing a well needed deflection before restarting the conversation she was having with Julia. "So, Julia, did you manage to get him to let you pop his shoulder back in, or was he being a total douchebag about it?"

I start to walk away, wondering who they were talking about, especially when I heard Julia add that whoever it was had let her do it while crying like a baby but then promptly passed out.

I make a beeline for the hotel lift. I know Mars said in the message to meet him in an hour, but I'm extremely conscious that I've been sat in tight jeans throughout the whole game, on a plastic seat. God knows how sweaty I am down there, and I'm not going to risk that it might smell anything other than fresh. Plus, although I'd not even thought about it, last night when Mars had been doing all those delicious things to me, I'm not sure how tidy everything is either. I know my arm pits could do with a once over.

The underwear I'm wearing is far from sexy too, but I have the perfect 'you never know when a girl's going to get lucky' matching set of lingerie, that I'd dropped into my overnight bag before we'd left Billings.

As soon as I step into the room, and the door closed behind me, I strip out of my clothes, bundling them all up, and shoved them on the floor at the side of my open suitcase. All except the Longhorns top, which I lay neatly on the bed. The shower is hot, but not too hot that my skin will get too flushed. Turns out that everything is pretty trimmed but my pits do have a smidgen of growth, so I lathered up and run a razor over the skin there.

Dried off and feeling so much fresher, I dress in the royal blue balconette bra and matching knickers. The fabric is so sheer it looks like a haze over my skin rather than material. They leave nothing to the imagination. Instead of wearing my tight jeans, I pull on a pair of black leggings instead, they're much comfier and less restricting. A quick reapply of minimal makeup, I tie up my hair exactly as it was before I'd hit the shower and I'm almost ready, looking as I did forty-five minutes ago.

You see, I don't want to look any different, otherwise Mars will think that I've gone to a lot of effort to impress him. Don't know why, but this is early days. If I get dressed up to the nines, then it's like I'm purposely vying for his attention, and I don't want him to get that impression.

Yeah, yeah. I've put naughty underwear on for the whole purpose of enticing him, and getting him all sexed up, but he'll only get to see it if I decide that he can.

The switch from jeans to leggings? Come on, black pants are black pants when it comes to men noticing what a woman is wearing.

The alarm goes off on my phone from when I'd set it for one hour earlier while waiting for the lift to reach my floor, so I click it off. With my Longhorns jersey back on, I take a last look in the mirror, tucking a stray hair from my ponytail behind my ear before making my way out, all the while checking that no one is around to see me.

When I manage to make it to the lift, insert the keycard and press the correct floor, I let out a deep sigh having made it this far without been seen. I take in a deep breath to try control the nerves that are doing a highland fling in my stomach.

CHAPTER 29

Not sure whether to knock or use my keycard to let myself in, I decide to do both; a quick light rap on the door and scan my card. Before I have a chance to push at the door, it opens.

He's stood in the doorway, still dressed in jeans and a t-shirt, but he's barefoot and smiling at me like the cat that's got the cream.

He doesn't say anything, but his arm scoops around my waist and he pulls me into the room, quickly closing the door behind me.

My back hits the door mere seconds after his mouth covers mine, and he's kissing me. Hot, demanding kisses, which tell me exactly how much he wants me. While his mouth devours me, his hands are everywhere. In my hair, fingers trailing down my neck, tracing the V-neck of my sports top.

"Glad you kept the top, but I'm disappointed that you've not got my number on your back," he murmurs against my lips.

"That might be because I haven't yet decided if you're

my favorite player or not," I gasp breathlessly, shocked by his delicious assault.

"Believe me, Hope. When it comes to you, I sure as hell ain't playing." He nips at my bottom lip before he sucks it into his mouth. "When it comes to you, I'm deadly fucking serious." While he trails his tongue and hot wet lips across my jawline, and down my throat, sucking at my skin that covers my pulse, I hold on to his biceps to keep me upright. Heat soars through me when his hand starts to move, slipping under the hem of my jersey, his fingertips stroking over my stomach before cupping and squeezing my breast.

"God, you smell so fucking good. I'm glad you ditched the tight jeans and changed to leggings instead. Far easier to take off." So much for him not noticing. Before I know it, he has the waistband clutched in his fists and he's peeling them down my legs. When he gets to the ankle, he drops to his knees. He makes quick work at getting rid of my trainers, lifting my foot before flipping it off. Considering that he's seems to be super eager to get me naked, there's a gentleness about it.

"Wait," I gush out, and he stops dead, still holding the second trainer in his hand. "The card for my room is in there, don't lose it."

"You keep stuff in your shoe?" he looks puzzled.

"Not normally," I giggle, "Usually I put it in my bra but…" Damn, Here I am trying to be cool, and I've just admitted that I was preempting him groping my tits, so had left out any extra baggage in my bra.

"Thank fuck for that," Mars launches the trainer over his back. My leggings, now free from my legs, quickly follow and then he's hooking my leg over his shoulder. "For a minute, I thought you were going to stop me from doing this," His mouth is on my pussy, sucking at me through the sheer fabric. "Nice panties, but so not sorry," he growls as he grabs the fabric, and tears it with his hands, "I need you bare to me."

"Oh, bugger," I squeal out when he flicks my clit with the tip of his tongue.

The next second, he's got both my legs over his shoulders and a firm grip on my arse, taking my full weight while somehow getting off his knees and coming up to his full height. I hold on tight to his shoulders, my upper body arched so I don't hit the ceiling, and he carries me across the room to the large fabric couch. But instead of sitting on it, he sits on the floor, his head tilted back against the seat cushion, his mouth still sucking and licking on my pussy. My knees hit the edge of the couch seat. With one strong hand, fingers sinking into the flesh of my bum, he holds me there. With his other, he takes mine, placing it onto the back of the seating, giving me that extra support and balance. "I need to taste you deep inside, feel your sweet, warm flesh against my tongue." His grip on my bum brings me even closer to his face, the tilt of his head giving him the perfect angle so he can spear me deeply with his tongue while still managing to breathe.

I'm literally riding his face, my hips rock against him as he gives me a full-on tongue fucking.

He no longer has to keep me firmly in place because, quite frankly, I ain't going nowhere, his hands are all over my arse, but this time he's kneading, caressing, with his huge palms. Out of nowhere, he draws back his hand and slaps my cheek at the same time as he withdraws his tongue, and presses it hard against my already swollen clit. I shriek out in surprise, and when he laughs the vibration against my pussy lips sparks all sorts of delicious sensations that shoot to my core.

Another quick smack in the very same spot, the tips of his fingers slip between my pussy lips and run the length from clit to puckered hole. "Let me here?" his deep and pleading voice, as if desperate to go that one step further, vibrates against my swollen bud. "Let me finger you here, make you come so hard that you'll never forget me again."

"Mars?" I say hesitantly. Only once before have I let someone play with my arse like that, and let's just say, he was far too eager and didn't take the time to get me all riled up first. It was a disaster. A very painful disaster, and one I didn't want to repeat. Although, Mars has got me so wet, so bloody horny, that the thought of it makes me almost crave his further exploration. "Yes," I hum. "Yes, Mars. I need to come so bad…"

"You beautiful, sexy, dirty girl," he growls, grabbing my hips and moving me down his body until I'm sat on his upper thigh. The outline of how hard he is for me is clearly visible under the fabric of his jeans. "I need to be inside you, and I want no barrier, I want to take you bare. I swear to you I'm clean. Are you…?"

"Yeah, I'm good, I'm on birth control."

"Then take my cock out." I don't hesitate, popping the button at the waistband, releasing the zip until I can see the tempting line of hair that leads to where I'm heading. Sliding my hand beneath the fabric, I release his hard erection fully before curling my fingers around it. The skin of the head of his cock is so silky yet hot, The shaft, hard as rock. The vein underneath stands proud all the way to a perfectly sized pair of balls. He's certainly not lacking in length, girth or the nut sack department. With one hand holding him firmly, and with his help, I push the top of his pants down his hips to his thighs, where I lift myself up and reposition myself until the swollen head of his cock is pushing against the entrance of my pussy. I don't rush it, but I don't fuck about torturing him either. I drop down onto him, a sob at the feeling of fullness escapes my open lips.

"Oh… yes," Mars cries with a gasp at the sensations coursing through his body from the feel of being fully seated inside me. "God, you feel so good, so tight, you're so fucking perfect." His arms reach around me, one hand snaking between my arse cheeks, down to my pussy where he must be able to feel his shaft as it glides in and out of me. His fingers, now slick from the wetness there, move back towards my arse hole, working it around, dipping the very tip into my puckered hole. When his fingers push in a little further, I feel the burn, but with a gentleness, he works his way further inside me, and the pain very quickly becomes something totally different, making me wonder how it would feel if it was his cock there. Making me realise it's something I'm definitely up for exploring.

With his finger in my arse, his cock sliding in and out so deep, our bodies clash together as we seek a deeper penetration. It's not long before I'm panting, heart racing and my vision becomes blurry as I start to shake, hurtling towards my orgasm. A scream of pleasure bursts from my lips when it hits, and I slump forward over Mars, unable to keep myself upright. Mars doesn't let up. With a quick flip, I'm on my back, Mars gripping my hips with his firm hands as he continues to power into me, seeking his release. When I see that he's so close, still a little dazed, I reach a hand up to him, pulling him down to me and place my lips on his perfect mouth. When he takes my kiss with equal eagerness, I suck his lip into my mouth and bite.

The growl that bursts from deep within him, as his body pulses with desire, is purely carnal. Perfection all wrapped into one hot and enticing fine piece of arse, and despite only just reconnecting, the way he's looking at me through deep, dark and lust-fueled eyes, tells me that this is more than sex or trying to catch up on the last few years that were not meant to be. This is something so much more. Much more than those fledgling feelings that we first encountered at a cheap hotel in Sheffield.

As if to prove a point, Mars kisses me with so much fiery passion that I'm left breathless and wanting more. And from the words and promises that Mars whispers to me as he places tiny kisses across my skin, I know it's going to be a long night.

A very long, heated and beautifully exhausting night.

CHAPTER 30

The trip back to Billings had gone as planned. Both Mars and I kept a respectable distance from each other, but not without intermittently heated glances.

Mars has been turning up to every counselling session that he's been rostered to attend, but as yet, we haven't got past flicking the lock on the door and taking advantage of the privacy. On one occasion, when he'd turned up stressed after a heated difference of opinion discussion with the defence coach, I convinced Mars to let me give him a deep muscle massage. The plan was to alleviate his stress. Mars had other ideas on how he could do that, and quickly it turned out that it was me laid out on the table on my back while he pounded into me. We both got our stress well and truly released that day.

But enough is enough. This can't continue.

However much the sex is mind-blowingly good, the session we have scheduled for the actual therapy is what we need to be focused on, and that alone. It's not like we don't see each other away from club grounds. Most nights we spend together, we eat, and we chill watching re-runs of classic NFL games. Most of the time, it's at my condo, but when we have full free days, we steal away somewhere there's less chance of us being seen together, then usually end up back at his stunning four bed home a few miles out of town. The evenings inevitably end with incredible sex, sometimes a little rough, but in the best possible way. Other times he makes slow, passionate love to me that ignites so much emotion that we end up clinging to each other, blown away by the crazy connection between us that only seems to intensify. In the early hours of the morning, we slip back to our respective homes, only to arrive at work with our mask firmly in place, totally apathetic towards one another in front of the players, and our work colleagues.

So last night, I played the no sex card. Unless Mars promised that when he turned up for his session today, number bloody nine might I add, and nearly four weeks since I arrived here, he would take it seriously. Otherwise, my body was out of bounds. After some consideration, he'd agreed.

It's time to get to the bottom of Mars' behaviour, despite there being nothing new in the press recently. Which if there were, it would definitely be fake or old news. I have access to his schedule and know when he has training, meetings and when he gets his downtime. All his free time that he does get, he spends with me. So, I'm one hundred percent sure that I'm the only girl he's been fooling around with, and so far, we've managed to avoid any media attention.

Sat ready in my office, I wait for Mars to arrive. Everything is set up exactly as it was on the second attempt on that first day, after the ice bath fiasco. His file is open resting in my lap, my recording device is on the small table in front of me, along with a jug of iced water and two glasses.

A firm rap of knuckles on the door has me lifting my head and calling out for him to come in. The door swings open, and I inhale sharply.

Mars is every bit the strong, hard-hitting NFL player when he's wearing his football kit, he makes my temperature rise, but when he's dressed as he is now. I never thought I'd say this but, he's way hotter than Hardy. More captivating than Cavill, and a damn site dirtier than Dornan, which by his whispered promises in the heat of the moment, I can attest to.

Beckham, back off beautiful. There's a new sports sex god in town, and his balls are diamond-encrusted platinum.

What is it about men in sweatpants? Grey is good, but holy fuck, the black pair he's wearing low on his hips are doing all sorts of naughty things to my lady bits, and with the tight, white, ab-hugging t-shirt he's added, he is smoking hot. I'm sure he's dressed like this intentionally, hoping I'll be the one breaking the no-sex agreement.

"Come sit, Marshall." I gesticulate with my hand to the seating available opposite me. Mars bypasses the armchair, this time picking the more comfortable options of the couch.

"Are we really going to do this?" he asks with a smirk on his face, patting the seat beside him. "Are you sure you don't want to hop on up here with me so I can finger your pussy?"

"You promised, Marshall," I reprimand, making sure I don't use the name Mars, as it's less official, and at this moment, I need to keep this professional. Although my body sure as hell isn't getting with the program. Keeping my voice stern, I continue. "You need to take me seriously; we can't avoid this any longer."

"Yeah, yeah. I know," he sighs out, rubbing his hands nervously over the fabric of his sweatpants. "I'm just not sure what it is that you want to know. You know me already, so…"

"Sure, I know a little about you when we were at the same school together. I have an idea of how your life progressed from then until now, but if you really think about it, I don't know very much about you at all."

"So, ask me a question," he throws up his hands in defeat. "Anything at all?"

"Fair enough. Let's start then," I hesitate for a minute, before shooting the first question at him that will take him back to the very beginning, and hopefully giving me a true understanding of his life. "So, were you born in Yorkshire?"

Mars blows me away, because now I have him talking, he opens up quite freely about his childhood. How, up until he'd won his scholarship to move to the States, he'd never been out of Yorkshire. Which I immediately thought was strange because, as far as I can remember, Mars' family wasn't short of money, he always had use of a banging car and the most up-to-date, costly sports gear.

"Didn't you ever go on trips, holidays abroad with your parents?"

With the mention of his parents his demeanour changes instantly. There's a tightness in his jaw, furrowed brows, and a flushness to his skin. A storm rages in his eyes with an intensity that I've not seen before. Straightening up from what had been a relaxed pose on the couch, he sits forward, forearms resting on his thighs, fist clenched hard, knuckles white, as if imagining someone's head is placed in his palm. His Adam's apple bobs in his throat, telling me that he's doing all he can to swallow down his emotions.

"My parents were a joke," he hisses out between clenched teeth. "They didn't have the ability to look after a goldfish, never mind a kid. You know who looked after me until I was thirteen?" He asks, poignantly. "A constant stream of nannies and au pairs, and even they left eventually." No longer seated, Mars is up on his feet, pacing the floor behind the couch. "My parents didn't give a toss about me. They thought their parental responsibility was leaving a bunch of cash on the kitchen counter before taking off again for another business trip."

Wow. Oh Wow. Now we're getting somewhere. Sure, I picked up on the fact that back when we were at school, Mars always seemed to be different to the other football lads he hung around with. Although part of the team, he had an air of independence about him. And come to think of it, when we'd spent that night in the hotel together, he had mentioned his parents were out of town and his older siblings were living in a different country.

"What you're saying is that your parents weren't around much during your childhood due to their work?"

"Work, if you call spending a couple of hours in meetings, then spending the rest of the week living the high-life in places like Monaco, Vegas or on some luxury yacht in the Bahamas."

"Didn't they ever take you with them?" I question,

because surely, they must have spent some time with him. Was this just a key latch kids' impression of what their childhood was like, or was this his reality?

"Jesus, Hope. They'd turn up out of nowhere, giving it the big, 'Our boy, we've missed you so much' playing the role they thought they needed to in front of the hired help. I'd ask, no beg for them to take me with them the next time. But every time they had a reason, an excuse to why they couldn't. Every single one feeble. So, you see, the next time never came." He drops back down on the couch, dropping his head into his hands, his shoulders sagged, and waves of mental exhaustion flow from him.

It's unbelievable. While my childhood was stifled with an overly obsessive father, Mars was given next to no parental attention, and zero sense of love or stability.

I want to shout and scream out how utter pillocks his parents were, hold him tight and tell him how he was deserving of so much more, but instead I keep my anger under wraps. For now, anyway.

"So, I know this question might seems stupid to you, but can you describe what your day-to-day life was like back then."

Mars, goes on to explain how it was a revolving door of nannies, and au pairs coming and going. It was their job to chauffeur him to and from school, and make sure he was clean, fed and got enough sleep on a night. Any of them he did strike up a bond with and became close to, it wasn't long before they left too. When he got to fifteen, the au pairs were swapped for house keepers, who would make sure that everything in the house was in order but would leave by the end of the working day, leaving Mars alone by himself in the huge house.

"Football's what got me though. That and the guys.

Yes, I know you think Bell and the guys were total dickheads. What was it you called us? FUB's," he laughs, but it's far from a happy one. "Fucking uneducated ballbags," I clarify with an embarrassed grimace.

Shaking his head, he becomes all serious again. "But they stuck by me. The guys, Coach Blackmore and football were the only constant in my life, and exactly what I needed."

I had no clue. I had no clue what had been going on in his life.

When he'd opened up to me in the hotel, I'd seen the real Vance Marshall. I'd seen a young man who, despite hiding behind a stoic expression and unexpressive actions, was kind, gentle, funny and caring. A man who cared for me, who had shown his feelings to me openly.

And what did I do?

I left him.

A man who struggled with abandonment issues and was deprived of love.

I drop his file on the table in front of me and get to my feet. In a matter of seconds, I'm sat on the couch beside him.

"Mars," I whisper. "I had…"

"Hope," Coach Scully's voice boomed from the doorway as it flew open. As soon as he saw us both sitting on the couch, he halted in his tracks. "Oh, shit, I didn't know you were in here, Marshall."

"We're in the middle of a session, Coach, this is not a good time," I reprimand, annoyed that he's interrupted us at a critical moment.

"Sorry, sorry I'll make it quick," Coach brushes it off like it's not really that much of an issue he's walked in at a poignant moment. "I checked with the powers that be, and they said it's totally fine for Lucy to move into the apartment with you, as long as she understands it's only until your contract is up at the end of the three-month term. See you later at the Hot Yoga class." And with that he's gone.

I turn my attention back to Mars, placing my hand over his that is resting on the couch by his side. As soon as my palm touches his skin, he snaps his hand away and once again jumps to his feet.

"Mars, what's wrong?"

"What am I doing? Why am I letting you do this to me again?"

"What?" I fret, wondering what the hell has caused this sudden change in him. "I'm trying to help you."

"No, you're not. You've been leading me on, raking up all the feelings that I have for you, bringing them to the surface. Don't you fucking see it? You're messing with my head, messing with my heart and getting me to fall for you all over again."

It takes me a minute before I realise that Mars isn't referring to the therapy. He's talking about us.

"That's not true, I..."

"What's not true?" he says accusingly, "That you're not going to up and leave me? Like every other fucking person I cared about in my life."

"You always knew that my contract was only for three months." Although I shouldn't have to justify myself, my chest tightens as panic begins to rise within me. "I've never tried to hide that from you. You've known this from the start."

"Yeah well, stupid me, thinking that with how things have been going between us, how we'd reconnected, would have changed things. That for once in my life, someone might want me enough to feel that I'm worth sticking around for." He stomps across the floor to leave.

"You've got this all wrong, Mars." I reach out to him only for him to shake me off again. "Please let me explain," I plead as he pulls open the door.

"What's the point, Hope. You fooled me once, fooled me twice; you don't get to fuck me over a third time."

"Mars, please," I beg, but it's too late, he's gone.

CHAPTER 31

stand, statue like, and look at the closed door. The door that was just slammed in my face, giving me a clear message, I had royally fucked up.

Not now. Now was nothing compared to the major trauma I left behind when I penciled that note, taken my last look at the one person that saved me from a life of hell, and then left.

I might not have caused the hairline fractures that run through Mars' heart on that day, but I sure as hell made it crack a little further, and break a little more.

I always thought it was me that had been the broken one, but Mars is broken too, and I'd done nothing to help fix him.

If I'd have known how damaged Mars had been, would I have walked away from him? I don't honestly know. Look where he is now. Rising high and still has a future in football.

But I've hurt him. Hurt him so much.

Twice he has given me all of him. In his eyes, both times I have given him nothing in return.

We're back to that same old dilemma.

It's flight or fight time.

To me it's a no brainer, but before I get the chance to make a move, the door flies open again.

It's when Mars walks around me, and sits back down on the couch I realise I'm still standing in the same place when he left, only now my face is wet from the tears that had come with my frustration and devastation when he'd gone.

"You came back," I murmur, wiping the moisture from my face before I turn around and take the seat I had before, directly opposite him.

"You want to explain, now's your chance. Start talking," He's got that stubbornness about him that I faced at the very start. The walls that had disintegrated between us are firmly back in place. In his eyes anyway.

I take in a handful of deep, calming breathes before pleading my case.

"Yes, my contract with the Longhorns is only for three months and yes, I will be leaving, but because of my job Mars, not because of you." He huffs as if I'm talking shit, and I know I have to lay bare all my plans, my hopes and my truths.

"Mars, don't think for one minute the past few weeks have meant nothing to me. They mean everything. From the day I left you sleeping in that hotel room, I've felt regret, but it was the right thing to do. But now, things are different."

"You say that, but it doesn't stop you from pissing off, does it."

"No, I can't promise that I'll never have to leave you Mars, but I can promise that as long as you want me, I will be coming back," His brow creases, his eyes seek mine, looking for evidence that I'm speaking the truth. "When I finish here, my next contract is for six months with the Broncos. I've already agreed the terms, which means that I will only have to be on site three days a week. The rest of the time I'll be conducting my session via video call."

"So, what does that mean?" His voice is all gravelly and full of emotional anticipation.

"It means that four days a week, I'll need somewhere to live. Somewhere here in Billings, because Vance Marshall," I choke out, my voice thick with emotion. "I would rather die before walking away from you again." I can no longer stop the tears. I don't even want to. My true feelings are bared for him to see.

Mars stands slowly, his body language and facial expression gives nothing away.

"Come here," he says hooking a finger at me, beckoning me to go to where he stands. Although I'm a little unsure exactly how this is going to pan out, I go to him freely. How could I not? I want him. All I can hope is that he still wants me too.

I stand in front of him, my head tilted up so I can make eye contact with him.

"Mars, there will be times that we are apart because of your career and mine, but I can assure you I'll do my utmost to make it as minimal as possible. I'm as desperate for us not to be apart as you are, but I don't want us hating each other either, for giving up what we love."

My body shakes from the realisation that he could still reject me, and what I'm offering him is still not enough.

If it is not and he walks away, I would definitely be broken in two.

In a swift sharp movement, Mars' hands are in my hair, gently pulling until he has me exactly where he wants me. His head drops and his lips are on mine, kissing me, stealing my every breath until I'm whimpering with sheer lust and relief. With a hand on my arse, he lifts me, my legs wrap around his waist, my hands curl around his neck, wanting to hold on to him and not let him go.

"Move in with me," He murmurs against my lips. "Then at least when you are home, you're home with me."

"I'll need a space to work, without interruptions," I throw out my arms and giggle. My heart pounding with excitement and delight, my cheeks flare with heat. He's not turning me away.

"We have plenty of rooms. We can set you up your own designated office space, no problem," I kiss him hard on the lips, before flinging my head back and laughing out loud. "Is that a yes?" he asks, giving my bum a squeeze.

"How can I say no when you're already talking as if it's my home too? Yes, of course, I'll move in with you." I singsong. He swirls us both around in a circle until we're dizzy.

"There is one condition," he adds before dropping me down until my feet hit the floor.

"I haven't moved in yet and you're already setting down rules?" I squint eye him. "Hit me with it."

"We come out to the team, Coach, everyone, because I don't care about your stupid no mixing business with pleasure rule. The board will have to lump it. I'm sure they'll be only too pleased that I'll no longer be a free agent, and therefore giving the scandal mongers less dirt to splash on social media."

"Less?" I raise an eyebrow at him. "I hope you mean none."

"Can't guarantee that I might not misbehave and get you in a compromising position when we're out celebrating a win," he winks. "But I can guarantee it will only be you. It's only ever been you, and if the world knows that you're officially mine, then that's no scandal, that's romance."

EPILOGUE

"Well, Jeff. It's been another fantastic year in football and none more surprising than the Montana Longhorns championship win against the Pittsburgh Steelers."

"It sure was Cory, but when you look back over the season, you can't deny that the Longhorns are one of the most hard-working teams out there."

"So, true Jeff, so true. And with the Walter Payton NFL Man of the Year award going to the Longhorns Linebacker, Vance Marshall, and the AP Coach of the Year going to Raymond Scully, the club must be riding one hell of a high."

"You bet, Cory. When you check the stats for the individual players for example, Burress, Boiman, Barker, Conner and of course the Quarterback, Dallas Rucker, The Longhorns, have an impressive team and I can't wait to see what the next season brings for each one of them."

"Counting the days, Jeff. Counting the days."

. . .

Sat sidewards on the couch with my feet up, listening to the commentary through one ear pod as it comes to an end, my heart is bursting with pride at the high regard not just my man is getting but the whole team. The Longhorns had been marked as the outsiders to win the Super Bowl this year, but you should never rule out the underdog. Sure, the Steelers had been riding high in the NFL for years, but the Longhorns had worked their bloody socks off to rise in the ranks and deserved to be the ones to grab the title.

Sadly, I've watched the live game on the T.V. Lucy is here with me, keeping me company. Mars wanted me there but was adamant that he wouldn't put me at risk or the two tiny babies that are four weeks away from being full term.

I was gutted, especially as last season, The Longhorns had got so close to making it to the Super Bowl, only to be knocked out in the semi-finals but had gone all the way this year. But seeing as I look like I'm carrying a couple of footballs under my top, and my back is on a constant moanathon from the pressure, in some ways I'm glad that Mars insisted I stay at home and rest. I miss him.

So much has happened over the past fourteen months, one being getting knocked-up unexpectedly by the man I'm crazy in love with, and the only person I'd want to be the father to my babies. It's been a fast and furious ride.

One thing I've learned is that Mars is ruthless when he makes a decision, and as impatient as a five-year-old at an ice cream parlour. As soon as he'd finished kissing my face off at the therapy session where I'd agreed to move in with him, he had taken my hand and had all but dragged me along to Coach Scully's office.

My concern at provoking a backlash on exposing our new but compelling relationship was unfounded. Coach Scully had been sitting in his high-backed chair when Mars had rushed through the door without even knocking, me behind doing double time steps to keep up with him. In typical linebacker mode, Mars came in hard, defending me to the hilt, willing to take the hit for both of us. We were together, period, and it was non-negotiable.

Coach had raised an eyebrow, pulled his large frame up and out of the chair, shaking his head from side to side. "Thank fuck for that." Coach had blurted out with a laugh. "Can't say that I didn't see it coming. The sexual tension has been bouncing between the two of you from the moment I had you both in here bumping heads. It was as obvious as a one-legged man in an ass kicking contest." He went on to give Mars a lecture on getting his head out of his ass and doing right by me, followed with a stern warning about how he was going to beat the crap out of him if he didn't.

Coach took it to the board, who like Mars, had predicted, let out a deep sigh of relief at the prospect of their star linebacker not having shameful articles splashed across the media every week.

The team took the piss out of Mars, and no one was more surprised than me when his only reaction was to laugh with them, taking it on the chin. When I asked him how come he wasn't losing his shit, he kissed me until I was breathless, telling me why would he? He was the happiest he'd ever been, and now had everything he'd ever wanted.

The press had a field day with headlines of 'Love in the locker room' and 'Marshall's = Sex = Therapist'. That wasn't the worst, and I think they thought our relationship was just a flash in the pan. But when one of the journalists picked up on the fact we had gone to school together, out came the second chance romance headlines. The negative gossip soon died down, along with some old stories that had been purposely surfaced and pushed in front of my face in the attempt to get a rise out of me. It didn't work, and after a few public appearances together, our unequivocal connection there for all to see, it was all about the love and how we were the new IT couple in the sporting world.

On a positive press note, if it weren't for them, I would never get the story out of Mars as to what had happened to his phone for him to be acquainted with the guy who fixed my wet one.

Skinny dipping in the Scott Memorial Fountain in Belle Isle Park, Detroit after a cracking game against the Lions. Too much alcohol and a couple of jersey chasers were behind him, getting into trouble. Coach Scully and a very empathetic Detroit police officer were the ones who got him out of it.

My phone buzzes on the coffee table in front of the couch, and I place a hand on my swollen belly as I stretch over to grab it.

"Don't you dare!" Lucy shrieks at me, gently pushing back on my shoulder. I hadn't even seen her coming out from the kitchen where she'd gone to get me a drink of iced water. "You'll end up on the floor if you're not careful." Placing the drink on the surface, she pics up the phone and takes a quick glance at the caller I.D. "It's Baby Daddy." Lucy informs me, handing it over. She's been calling him that since the day I let her in on our secret. We hadn't told many people at the beginning, as we hadn't wanted to risk it getting leaked to the press before we'd managed to get our own heads around it. Twins. Never was I the type of person to do things by half.

Lucy walks towards my office, where she's been working from while staying with me. It's only until Mars gets back from Chicago, where the final was held this year. Lucy now lives in the condo that I was staying at when I first came to Billings. Not long after Mars and I got together, with a little encouragement from me, I convinced her to go for the PR job. In my eyes, if she was good enough to cover the position for the time that they expected, she was the perfect candidate for the job. She got it, and also managed to negotiate the apartment as part of her salary deal.

"Hey babe, how you are feeling?" Mars' deep, thrill-inducing voice vibrates down the phone. Damn, it gets me every time.

"Never mind me, I'm fine," Tears build in the corner of my eyes. Pregnancy does turn you into a soppy bugger. "Congratulations, I'm so fucking proud of you. I knew you and the guys could do it. Go Longhorns," I whoop out, fist pumping the air even though he can't see me. Ouch, that wasn't such a good idea.

"Hope, it was fucking incredible. The atmosphere in the stadium was indescribable."

"God, I wish I could have been there with you," I choke out. I try to hide it but, yeah, pregnancy.

"Are you sure you're, okay?" he asks again, his voice full of concern. "Is Lucy there with you?"

"Yes, she's here and, of course, I'm fine. I just miss you."

"I know baby, I miss you so fucking much, but I have

to hang around here tonight and do a shit ton of bollocks with the rest of the guys before I head home. I'll be back tomorrow around lunchtime," he assures me, even though I'm aware. I've been counting down the hours and minutes since he left.

"I know, I know and it's fine," I say with a fake upbeat tone. "Go, go do what you need to do and don't forget to take time out to celebrate with the guys. You deserve it." I hear someone in the background shouting Mars' name.

"Sorry babe, I gotta go." The frustration in his voice for having to cut the call short is clear. "I'll see you tomorrow."

"I'll be here waiting," I singsong, hoping he doesn't pick up on the crack in my voice when the words get stuck in my throat.

"Hey, Hope…" I wait, as he yells at someone to give him a minute. "I love you so fucking much. Bye, babe."

"I love you too, Mars. Bye." I wait until the call drops, then grip the phone to my breast, letting the tears fall freely.

Pathetic, that's what I am.

It's not like this is the first time we've had to spend time away from each other. Our work dictates it. We miss each other deeply, but when we are together, it's electric. The passion is off the scale. The sex is heady, a little needy and so fierce as we grasp and hold on tight to every second of it as we make up for every moment we're apart. But since the doctors' orders of no more flying or long-distance travel earlier than expected, I'd had to cut back on work. It also now clashed with the end of the football season, meaning I couldn't even attend the away games, leaving me out of sorts.

"Hey, what's up?" Lucy asks, seeing my tears when she comes out of the office to see what Mars had to say. "Baby Daddy hasn't got an injury, has he?"

"He's fine. I'm just being a stupid, pregnant, paranoid idiot," I sob.

"Paranoid?" she sniggers. "About what?"

"Well, look at me." I wave my hands up and down my bloated body. "I'm a big, fat blob of a mess."

"That's crap," Lucy snaps back. "You're a beautiful, blooming, pregnant woman who happens to be one of the kindest, funniest people I know, and I'm honored to call a friend." She sits on the edge of the couch and takes one of my hands. "You're not worried that Marshall is getting up to his old tricks, are you?"

"He could have relapsed." My heart thumps hard inside my chest, sweat beads on my forehead and top lip as panic rises at the thought of Mars even looking at another woman.

"Ha, are you joking? You've more chance of Donald Trump growing old gracefully and taking a new wife in the same age range as he is." Lucy doesn't hold back, her shoulders bobbing up and down as she laughs out loud at her own joke. "Baby Daddy is so infatuated with you; he'd never betray you. And he's a strictly two beers max kinda guy now too."

I don't respond; all I offer is a snort at her attempt to appease me.

"What did he say to you on the phone?" she urges, giving me hand a bit of a squeeze.

"He asked if I was okay." Lucy raises a brow, waiting for more. "Told me that he misses me."

"And?" she presses.

"That he loves me."

"Mhm… how much?"

"So fucking much," I snigger, realising how silly I'm being.

"Then what is all this about?" she raises her arms in the air in question. "Because one thing I'm sure of is that Vance Marshall doesn't lie to me, to his team, and certainly not you."

"I'm being stupid, aren't I?" Sighing deeply, I slowly swing my legs over and shuffle in my seat until I'm sitting upright.

"Not stupid," She does a couple of melodramatic blinks at me. "Crazy, yes. But not stupid."

"Cheeky bugger," I chuckle, swotting her on her arm.

"It's getting late and after all that crying, you must be exhausted. Why don't you go take a nice warm relaxing shower, get all cozy in bed, and get some sleep? Before you know it, it will be morning and only a couple of hours before Baby Daddy is home."

Lucy's right. I am exhausted. With my emotions running wild and having two growing babies to carry around inside me, it's no surprise, really. So, before taking myself off to my bedroom, I give Lucy a hug, and wish her goodnight, telling her I'll see her in the morning seeing how she's crashing in one of the guest rooms while Mars is away, keeping me company. Mars was adamant that he didn't want me to be on my own in case of an emergency.

The shower does the trick. The heat eases my back ache and soothes my bones. Once dried and dressed in one of Mars' t-shirts, I slip under the quilt and I'm asleep before I've let out my first relaxing sigh.

A warm hand with the gentlest of touch slips over my hip and up over my swollen belly. The featherlight contact is so delicate that, at first, I think I'm dreaming, until I feel the heat of his firm chest against my back. "Mars?" slips from my lips, voice thick with sleep. The room is lit by a shard of moonlight sneaking through the break in the curtains. "What time is it?"

"Shh," He moves up closer, wrapping me with his protective, strong arms. "It's a little after 1am baby, go back to sleep."

"Why are you home?" I tilt my head to the side so I can brush my lips against his cheek, but he preempts me perfectly, moving so his mouth meets mine with a sweet, gentle kiss.

"When I spoke to you earlier, I could hear it in your voice. You needed me home, so I grabbed an earlier flight."

"Mars, you didn't have to do that." I lay my hand over his, the one that is palm flat, caressing the bump that contains our children. "I was fine."

"Okay, truth," He brushes his lips against my temple, and across the bridge of my nose, before hitting me with a hot and passionate kiss to my mouth. "I wasn't okay. I was the one that needed to be home."

My heart squeezes tight. A spark of worry comes to the forefront of my mind. Mars has worked hard to exercise the effects left by the emotional trauma that he'd faced through childhood, but there's no guarantee that his fear of abandonment wouldn't rise again.

"Mars?" I question, bringing my hand up to his cheek. "Talk to me."

"It didn't hit me until the end of the game, how huge it was. We'd won the Super Bowl." He takes my hand from his cheek as he brings it to his mouth, kissing the palm. "One of the biggest events in my life was happening at that moment. The team was crazy excited. The fans were going wild, each and every one of them sharing the moment." His voice is thick with emotion and when a drop of wetness hits the back of the hand he's still holding, I realise he's crying.

"Mars," I roll to face him and get as close as possible, reaching up to place my hands on his cheeks. "I don't understand."

"But for me, it didn't feel right. Something was missing, and what was missing was you." A deep emotional sigh bursts from his mouth. "This time next year, once the season is over, I want us to get married," he vows. "No distractions. You, me, and the kids, together celebrating the most important day of our lives. Our family."

"Sounds perfect," I smile up at him in the dimly lit room.

"Hope, you're it for me. You always have been. We have so much to look forward to, special moments, and I do whatever it takes to make sure that I share every single one of them with you. I'll make it happen."

"Whatever it takes?" I suck in a deep breath and pant it back out.

"Anything. I love you so fucking fiercely that I'd take on the devil, if that's what's needed."

"No need for the devil," I grit out between clench teeth, wrapping my arm around my belly. "Mother fucking shit balls." I curse out on a deep exhale, as a pain so strong sears through my back and stomach. "Although you might want to shout for Lucy to bring the car out of the garage and grab my hospital bag from the downstairs closet."

"Holy fuck, Hope. Now?"

"I think when it comes to these two little balls of fun," I lovingly rub my hand over my swollen belly. "We're finally in the end zone."

THE END

ACKNOWLEDGMENTS

To my readers. Thank you for jumping into my crazy.

No author can do without the fabulous people that are their invisible scaffolding. So, I would like to give them a shout out and uber huge thank you.

My good friends and book loving queens, Jackie McLeish, Nikki Young and Lynn Allan. Extra shout out for Nikki for her hard work in looking after the reader group and casting the first eye over my WIP's.

Big thank you to Eleanor Lloyd-Jones and Caroline Stainburn for your excellent work. Without your expertise this book would be one hell of a shit show.

A special thank you to my pimpets and beta readers: Kirsty Adams, Helen Simpson, Victoria Philpott, Ann Walker, Joanne Edmunds, Lesley Robson, Nikki Robertson, Sarah Van Aker, Sophie Richards, Yvonne Eason and Wendy Susan Hodges. You all rock.

KL Shandwick, Ava Manello, and all my author friends for their support and many words of wisdom. Each one of you has helped me immensely. You are special people and I'm humbled by your kindness.

My reader group - T.L Wainwrights All Things Naughty Reader Group. Thank you for the feedback and support you have given me. Love you guys!

My family and friends both in and out of the book world.

ALSO AVAILABLE BY T.L WAINWRIGHT

Young Outlaws MC Series

Unlawful –book 1.

Justice - book 2.

Vengeance – book 3

Damaged Alpha Series

DEACON. Soldier. Fighter – book 1

TOMEK Saving angels – book 2

CHARLIE If only – book 3

JORDAN Broken Promise – book 4

Reed and Rice Series

Catching A Breath

Taking A Chance

Standalones

Dream F*#k's And Hard Drives

A Hole Lotto Loving

My Sweet Gi

Play for Me

YOU CAN FIND T.L HERE...

https://m.facebook.com/TL-Wainwright-137891269903535

https://www.amazon.co.uk/T.L-Wainwright/e/B012PBC6GC

Twitter: @wainwright_tl

Instagram: wainwright.tl

Bookbub: https://www.bookbub.com/authors/t-l-wainwright

Website: https://tlwainwrightreads.uk

Email: ttdwainwright@gmail.com

Printed in Great Britain
by Amazon